To Love and to Perish

Felicity Philips Investigates

Book 1

Steve Higgs

Dedication

This book is dedicated to Rolf Lawson for suggesting the title. Thank you, Rolf.

Table of Contents

Complicated Business

I asked, 'What was that?' The sound of something breaking upstairs had just stopped our discussion. We were midway through the bride making it clear her bouquet had to be pink gerberas. She'd gone so far as to specify the exact shade of pink, providing a swatch to make sure I would get it right.

Tamara Bleakwith was not unusual in my experience. Most brides have desires that might seem trivial to anyone else but are of paramount importance to them on their big day. She was really very pretty and the pictures I had seen of her fiancé showed a tall, handsome man – they were going to be a photogenic couple. She was petite, like me, with perfectly straight sandy blonde hair that fell almost to her tiny waist.

The bride and her mother were both on their feet, looking up at the ceiling. They both had deep frowns on their faces.

After what sounded like a vase hitting the oak floorboards above us, silence followed. Not for long though. It was interrupted by the sound of loud voices which echoed through the house as two men began arguing. I knew who the men were. One was the bride's father, Derek Bleakwith, and the other was John Ramsey, Derek's business partner.

'Please excuse us for a moment,' begged the bride's mother, Joanne Bleakwith. She looked embarrassed by the outburst I could hear and rushed from the room, her daughter following close behind.

Left alone in their house, I took a moment to go back over my notes so far. I travel with a tablet these days, having abandoned my notebooks no more than a couple of years ago. I found the leather and paper smell of the notebook comforting in a way, but the tablet was more practical, and it allowed me to send notes directly from it as a message or an email and that saved time.

The bride (and of course her mother who was doing a lot of steering) was to be married at Coolbridge Castle, in Lenham in twelve weeks' time. The venue is a popular location for weddings and thus one with which I am familiar. My familiarity helped, but this was still a rush job - twelve weeks is about the fastest I have ever organised a wedding. The haste was not due to the bride being pregnant as you might have imagined, but because her father was gravely ill.

My name is Felicity Philips, and I am a wedding planner. Actually, I like to think of myself as THE wedding planner and even use that line in some of my advertising. I have a rival who would argue the point, but by and large, I am the first port of call for those with money or fame.

At fifty-five I find myself a widow. It is not what I expected from life but tell myself one can only play the hand one is dealt. I am short and petite and have raven black hair from Italian heritage. I managed to luck out on the children front but have my niece as an assistant. She is nineteen, nimble, and has watched *The Karate Kid* far too many times.

I share my life and house with a Ragdoll cat called Amber and an English bulldog named Buster. They hate each other with passion. So much so, in fact, that I dare not leave them alone in the house together which is why Buster is currently snoring by my feet.

The cat and the dog ... no I'll start that again. I was going to say there is something unique about them, but in truth I think the oddity is me. I can hear their thoughts and understand them when they bark or meow. I had the ability from birth, I think. It caused me problems as a child because I didn't know I wasn't supposed to tell people about it. It's not all animals I can hear, just those I share my life with. At least, that is what I have come to believe. I got Buster and Amber after I lost my husband and started hearing their 'voices' not long after.

I have to tune them out when anyone else is around which might sound easy but is something I often struggle with.

My train of thought snapped back to the here and now when I heard Joanne's voice echo through the ceiling. She asked what was going on.

'You need to talk some sense into him,' John raged.

'Please lower your tone,' Joanne requested politely.

Her calmness only poured petrol on the fire. Raising his voice, John snapped, 'Derek needs to sign this paperwork and he is refusing.'

'Yes, John,' replied Derek, his voice quiet and weak to the point that I could only just hear his words. 'I know how highly you value Tarquin, but I am not ready to entrust the firm to him. Not yet.'

'You are no longer at the helm, Derek. You need to make Tarquin the CEO so that the company can move forward!' John was shouting again, but the tone of his words made it sound like a desperate plea.

'Why?' Derek wanted to know. 'Why such a desperate hurry? What difference does it make to you?'

John's voice was an angry roar. 'Just sign the paperwork!'

Derek replied in his weak voice. 'I am not dead yet, John. Regrettably, the current course of treatment is not having any more impact than the last one or the one before that.' His statement caused a few moments of silence. 'I will fight on, but the doctor cannot establish what is causing my condition. All he can do is grant me painkillers. However, my brain still works, and I can manage to run the firm from my bed. As principal shareholder, you can appoint Tarquin as my replacement if I die. I will not sign my firm away while I am still breathing, even to a man as talented as my future son-in-law.'

John didn't shout his response, but it sounded like a threat, nevertheless. 'This is a mistake, Derek. I cannot wait. I won't wait.'

'Why?' Derek wanted to know. 'What pressure are you suddenly under?'

If John gave an answer, I didn't hear it. The sound of heavy footfalls echoed across the ceiling above as someone (presumably John) stomped away.

I didn't mean to eavesdrop, I really didn't, and felt guilty that I could hear every word. The Bleakwiths lived in a wonderful sixteenth century farmhouse. The walls and ceiling were a little wonky, as one often sees with old houses. In the kitchen, I had spotted the familiar bow of a ship's hull in one of the beams. When broken up, parts of old warships were often repurposed for housebuilding. That was particularly true in this part of the world so close to Chatham Naval Dockyard where so many of the Navy's ships were built.

I know both Derek and John from school. You might say we grew up together. However, where Derek and I were friends – I was organising his daughter's wedding free of charge - John Ramsey and I did not see eye to eye. John was a nasty boy at school and though he might have changed as he aged, I never felt inclined to find out. I hated him back then and avoided him now.

Derek ran a successful printing business which he built from scratch. It's where I get all my printing done and I don't get charged because I am a silent partner in the firm. I invested some seed money thirty years ago when Derek was setting it up. The plan was to pay me back, but Derek suggested I keep a share instead. It has provided a dividend every year since which has repaid the original loan many times over.

I don't play a part in the firm, or attend any meetings though Derek always sends me an invite and a copy of the minutes. Had I been active, I might have tried to block John joining the firm a year after Derek started it.

I knew Derek was sick and had been for some time. It was something to do with his skin and he was suffering crippling joint pain too. I hadn't seen him for more than a year – busy lives and all that – when the call came from him to ask if I would arrange his daughter's wedding.

How could I refuse?

The heavy footfalls were now on the stairs, and curious (never nosey), I craned my head slightly to look back through the house.

John Ramsey's face was a mask of rage, colour filling his cheeks still as if he might be ready to burst like an overripe berry. Yanking his coat from the hook by the door, he tore the lining inside it, and swearing, stuffed his arms into it as he barrelled from the house.

The solid oak door slammed back into its frame with enough force to shake the house. It caused a fine sifting of dust to fall from the oak beams above my head.

Upstairs, the conversation continued yet now it was a soft muffled mumbling I could hear, the house doing its job to damp out the volume so the words could not be overheard.

Buster snorted, twitching in his sleep as he chased something imaginary in his head. I scratched his belly with a free hand, passing time while waiting for Tamara and Joanne to return and my thoughts drifted to the same subject they always did recently – the eagerly expected royal wedding. Twelfth in line to the throne, and soon to be pushed further back down the list as his eldest brother's wife was expecting yet another baby, Prince Markus was in possession of a twenty-five-thousand-pound diamond engagement ring.

How do I know that? Because the London jeweller that sold it to the prince's valet was good enough to let me know. I have a lot of friends and we help each other in a mutually beneficial manner.

The engagement had not yet been announced but I was manoeuvring myself into position because I wanted to plan that wedding. It would be the pinnacle of my career and an opportunity to do some of the things I had never been able to before. Previous royal weddings had been held at Westminster Abbey with all planning undertaken by the palace. The belief was that this one would be different. Prince Markus had very little to do with the royal family, choosing to live as normal a life as he could manage.

My daydreaming ended when I heard more footsteps on the stairs. Joanne and Tamara were returning, filled with apology, of course.

'I'm so sorry you had to hear that,' said Joanne with a sigh. I felt a natural inclination to pretend I hadn't heard anything, but she added, 'We all know how sound travels in this house.' Abruptly, she staggered and had to grab the wall to stay upright.

Tamara rushed to help. 'Mum, you know you shouldn't try to lift things.' Tamara looked my way and rolled her eyes. 'Mum helped dad get back into bed.'

Joanne winced, clearly in pain.

Tamara explained. 'Mum has a nasty spinal injury from a car crash in her twenties. It stopped all her sporting aspirations.'

Joanne groaned and shrugged her left shoulder as if doing so would lessen the discomfort she felt. 'Some days I can barely move. Tamara is right. I shouldn't lift things. Using my arms for anything more than some light gardening is too much.'

'How is Derek?' I asked, thinking it might help to change the subject. We'd been ignoring the topic since I arrived, but now I felt I had to ask.

Joanne sighed. 'The treatment isn't working, and his doctor is running out of things to try. His skin is terrible, and his joint pain keeps him awake. He says he can run the firm but in truth the painkillers he takes render him unable to do anything. He sleeps a lot.'

A tear fell from Joanne's left eye as she stared at the carpet.

Also tearful, Tamara put an arm around her mother, cuddling into her for comfort as they sat side by side on the couch opposite me. In a quiet voice, she revealed, 'It's why Tarquin and I want the wedding so soon.'

I knew that already, of course. 'Perhaps I ought to return later,' I suggested. This was a private moment on which I now felt I was intruding. Uncomfortable, what I wanted to do was escape. I had space in my diary most days this week to arrange a fresh appointment.

'No,' Joanne shook herself, reaching for a tissue to dab at her eyes. 'No, Felicity, I'm sorry for our emotional outburst. You are here and it would be unfair to make you return another time.' It really wasn't a big deal, but before I could say that she defeated me by saying, 'I believe Tamara and I would feel better knowing the wedding was on track.'

'Very well.' With a smile, I tapped the screen on my tablet, bringing it to life once more. 'We got as far as flowers.'

The meeting at their house continued for almost an hour. During that time, we arranged appointments at two bridal shops, a visit with Chef Dominic for cake tasting, and a meeting with the priest who would perform the ceremony.

When I left their house, Buster towing me along with powerful strides of his stubby legs, my thoughts were on what I needed to do next. Buster needed a walk after nearly two hours inside the Bleakwiths' house and was trying to stop to lift his leg on the way to my car.

'No, Buster,' I insisted, tugging him along.

'*But I need to go now,*' he whined.

'I'll take you to the park.'

'*It's not going to wait that long. I need some long grass if you get what I am saying.*'

I knew only too well, but I wasn't going to let him utilise the Bleakwiths' slightly overgrown lawn, that was for certain. He could hold it long enough to get out of their property and along the lane a little, or so I told him as I quickened my pace.

It was full autumn now, the trees devoid of leaves save for the scant few that clung on to their branches dearly though they were already brown and dead looking. The temperatures were dipping too, though it was warmer today and a lightweight coat was sufficient to keep the chill from my skin.

Once out of their gate, Buster decided enough was enough, *watering* the first dead weed he came to.

A car was coming along the lane toward me. Out here in the countryside, there are no pavements, so I stepped onto the grass verge to give it enough room to pass. As it turned out, the car veered off before it reached me, the driver steering through the double width vehicle entrance and into the Bleakwiths' drive.

Surprised, I recognised John Ramsey behind the wheel. He was back already though perhaps he was here to apologise for his earlier tantrum. Reminding myself that it was none of my business and tugged along by Buster, I headed down the lane, questioning whether I had indeed packed a baggie in my pocket.

We returned some ten minutes later with the intention of getting on our way. I was due to meet with Justin Cutler, my master of ceremonies, to go over the Hepworth-St George wedding planned for next weekend. We were going to have a late lunch at the Vaults in Rochester High Street.

When I heard the scream, I wondered if perhaps I might be late.

I took a faltering step, my feet moving toward the house automatically as a response to the scream before my brain took the reins and asked what I proposed to do. I'm a wedding planner for goodness sake. Was I going to kick down the door and take charge of the situation?

Last weekend at Loxton Hall I'd found myself fighting a crazed, knife-wielding killer. That I escaped relatively unscathed was a miracle in itself and largely due to the timely arrival of a private investigator/private security man called Vince Slater. That particular wedding went from bad to worse and the ceremony never took place because there were other maniacs ready to commit murder after the first one was taken care of.

Somehow, though semi-famous local sleuth, Patricia Fisher, solved the case, I was involved from start to finish and was credited with helping. That world was not mine though. I didn't run toward danger with an accomplished ninja butler at my side, I hustled smartly away from it instead like any normal person.

Yet as my foot twitched toward my car, another scream lit the air and the front door burst open.

John Ramsey ran from the house, leaving the door wide open in his flight. I gawped as he dug in his pocket for his keys. There was an obvious conclusion and I willingly leapt to it – he'd just done something to Derek Bleakwith and now he was running from the scene!

Honestly, I don't know where it came from, but without thinking it through first, I ripped open the door to my Mercedes, yelled for Buster to get in and threw myself down into the driver's seat. There was one way in and one way out of the Bleakwiths' property and that was through the gate. Spitting gravel from my tyres, I backed up twenty yards and spun the steering wheel so my car blocked the exit completely. John could escape on foot, but he wasn't driving anywhere.

I had the driver's door open the whole time, and no seatbelt on. Leaning out with my head cranked around to see where I was going, I was acting like some kind of stunt driver. My free hand did its best to pin Buster in place on the passenger seat and got slobbered on because that's what he does to show affection. My left shoulder protested – I managed to dislocate it a week ago and though it was healing, it wasn't exactly happy about being used.

I yanked the handbrake on and slammed my door shut just as John Ramsey drove at me. My heart almost stopped when my brain performed a swift velocity and distance calculation to say I was about to get rammed.

Instead, he slammed on his brakes, sliding across the gravel to stop a few inches shy of my window. The bonnet of his Range Rover filled my vision, and the blast of horn deafened my ears. He backed the horn up with angry profanity, swearing at me to move out of his way.

I scooted across the central transmission tunnel, hooking my dress so it wouldn't catch on the gear stick. Shoving the passenger door open, I said, 'Out, Buster. Let's go!'

'We only just got in,' he pointed out. 'Where are we going now?'

'Felicity needs to get out!' I gave him a shove, which didn't have a great deal of impact. Buster is basically a medium sized bean bag shaped sort of like a squat dog. If dogs were made of steel ball bearings that is, because he weighs about half a ton.

I gave up trying to get him to move and clambered over him, almost tumbling when I finally got my leading foot outside.

11

John was still shouting obscenities in my direction. He wanted to go, and his rage meter was in the red.

Of course, once I was out of the car, Buster thought we might be going somewhere interesting, so he got out too. I locked it quickly, grabbing Buster by his collar so we could get to the house.

However, John Ramsey was out of his car and he was mad. 'Give me the *something* keys!' he shouted, spittle flying from his lips. He didn't actually say the word *something* as you might imagine. I don't go in for bad language though so censored each word as they reached my ears.

'I'll let Buster go if I have to,' I warned. 'What did you do in the house? Did you hurt Derek?'

He didn't answer my question, what he said was, 'Give me the *something* keys or so *something* help me, I'll *something* you right up the *something*!'

His horrible mouth made me shudder. Where did people learn to talk like that?

I let Buster go with a swift command. 'Get him, Buster!'

It was only the dog making me feel brave, I can assure you. I'd never done anything this crazy before in my life, but as my dog tore across the three yards separating me from John Ramsey, I went to my right and across the front lawn to get to the house.

There were a score of windows at the front of the Bleakwiths' property, all possessing that beautiful leaded design that suited the old house and thatched roof perfectly. Any modern touches on a house like this would ruin the look. However, though I could see into the house, I could not see anyone moving about and a terrible thought occurred to me.

Had John just murdered all three of them?

My head swung back in horror, now terrified the man might have a knife or something. If he did, then he wasn't using it. He was on the bonnet of his car with Buster growling and barking from the ground. A larger dog would have jumped onto the bonnet in a single bound, but Buster would need a forklift truck to get that high.

Both were making a terrible racket; Buster barking maniacally, and John swearing in frustration at the dog who would not desist. Buster wanted the human to run away so he could give chase; that would be a fun game to play. John wanted to get into his car so he could run Buster over.

'Call him off, Felicity! Call him off now!' John bellowed his demands.

I shook my head and folded my arms. 'I don't think I shall, John.'

He sneered at me. 'You're enjoying this, aren't you? What? You think this is some kind of payback for me putting worms in your hair? Grow up, Felicity or I'll do much worse when I get down from here.'

I shook my head back and forth. Ever ready with a threat. He hadn't changed a bit since school. Well, he could try to get down and deal with me, but my money was on Buster. If John attempted to get off the car, he was going to get his ankles mauled to death. With that belief ringing in my ears, I ran to the house.

The front door was hanging open, I pushed through it and ran upstairs, confident John had hurt Derek and I would find Joanne and Tamara up there.

I was wrong though. I found the master bedroom easily enough, but it was empty. An additional single bed had been set up against one wall. The sheets were stained a little; Derek's terrible skin condition leaking plasma constantly. Next to his bed, a small table held cream and pills to treat his condition and a brandy decanter with two crystal glasses.

But where was Derek?

I heard voices outside and ran to the balcony. That it was open on a late autumn day was odd. The room was far too cool for a person to be comfortable in bed but looking over the edge of the balcony and into the garden, I saw a sight that took my breath away.

Derek was lying on the ground below. Half on the patio and half on the lawn, he wasn't moving and looked to be dead. Tamara was checking his pulse, one shaking hand to her mouth as the other felt his neck.

I pushed away from the balcony and ran back downstairs.

From where she stood in the kitchen, Joanne saw me reach the foot of the stairs and turn into the hallway. She shot me a surprised look but said nothing because she was on the phone to the emergency services. With her phone to her left ear, she was doing her best to explain herself to the person at the other end.

Terrified tears were streaming down her face.

Unsure what to do, I came up close to Joanne and waited. In the first ten seconds I heard what had happened.

'Yes, he pushed him!' Joanne cried into the phone. John hadn't returned to apologise for his earlier outburst. He returned to kill his partner. Joanne listened for a few seconds before adding. 'No, he's lying in the garden. No,' she sobbed. 'No, I don't know how badly he is hurt. He was already desperately sick. Dying we think.'

Feeling like I ought to be doing something to help, I left Joanne to continue talking on the phone and ran through the house to find Tamara. She hadn't moved since I saw her from above.

A sound behind me, made me jump but it was Tamara's mum, Joanne, returning. 'The police are coming along with an ambulance,' she announced, rushing around me to get to her husband.

I was a fifth wheel but as Joanne knelt beside her husband and daughter, I said, 'I blocked your driveway.' The two women swung their heads my way. 'I heard the scream,' I explained. 'So I used my car to stop him escaping. He did this?'

Tamara sobbed, holding her father's unresponsive hand, and it was Joanne's wavering voice that answered my question. 'We heard a shout and then this awful thump ...' she had to stop talking; the words just too painful to get out. She sucked in a lungful of air and tried again. 'It was like a sack of wet sand hitting the floor,' she sobbed, barely able to speak.

Abruptly, she stood up, a juddering huff of breath stilling her body as she looked away from her husband and back toward the still open patio door. 'You said you trapped him here?'

She wasn't really asking me to confirm my claim, nor was she waiting for an answer. She was stalking back through the house, heading for the front door, and pausing only to grab a brass candlestick from a mantlepiece on her way by.

I could only guess what she meant to do with it, and now torn between attempting to help Tamara with her stricken father, and stopping Joanne from doing something that would only make things worse, I chose the latter.

'Joanne!' I called after her, running through the house to catch up. 'Joanne, let's not do anything rash. You said the police were on their way.'

John Ramsey was still on the bonnet of his Range Rover. He was missing a shoe and the bottom three inches of his left trouser leg had been reduced to ribbons.

'*Come down*,' barked Buster.

'Call off your *something* dog!' John demanded, resorting to profanity yet again.

Joanne advanced across her gravel drive, a determination in her gait and the candlestick still gripped firmly in her right hand.

'Why?' she screamed. 'Why? You couldn't wait for natural causes to take him?'

'I didn't push him!' John shouted in reply. 'I already told you that!'

'You lied!' Mrs Bleakwith spat in response, the hand holding the candlestick twitching and shifting. I couldn't tell whether she was going to attack him or the car or both or neither. I also wasn't sure what I might be able to do to stop her if she did.

I'm five feet five inches and a hundred pounds plus some change. There just isn't a lot of me. Joanne had to be close to two hundred pounds and was six inches taller.

John Ramsey had an imploring look on his face when he said, 'Derek jumped, Jo. I'm telling you the truth. 'I don't think he could take the pain any longer. I came back to apologise, you know that.'

'I know what you told me,' Joanne made it clear she didn't believe him.

The sound of sirens in the distance drew our attention, all three of us straining our hearing to confirm what our ears believed.

'You can tell the police,' Joanne growled, throwing the brass candlestick to the ground.

John attempted to sidle to the edge of the car again, only to have Buster circle around and snap at him once more. There were scratches all over the car's previously immaculate paintwork where Buster had dragged his claws.

'Can you call off your dog, please?' John asked.

At least he managed to find some manners finally, but the answer was still a firm, 'No. I think Buster can keep you where you are for just a little longer. I'll call him off when the police get here.'

With a sense of acceptance, I backed away a pace and took out my phone. I needed to call Justin because I wasn't going to make it for lunch today.

A Challenge

It was cool enough outside for us to have been worried about Derek getting hypothermia. Leaving me to mind Buster as he in turn kept John on top of his car, Joanne and Tamara had gone to find blankets. He was still lying on the cold ground, but we didn't dare move him for fear of spinal injuries.

The police arrived just a few minutes later, their hurry to get to us probably aided by the ambulance ahead of them racing to save Derek's life. Both vehicles screeched to a stop in the lane beyond the Bleakwiths' gate, the people inside seeing the driveway blocked and coming on foot.

I would have to shift my car to let them park, but it could wait until John was in custody for sure.

The paramedics, first to arrive with heavy bags over their shoulders, bore questioning looks.

'In the back garden,' I supplied in a tone that demanded their haste. 'He's in bad shape,' I added to their backs as they ran for the front door.

Ten seconds behind them, two police officers came through the gates. They were both in their twenties – a tall, athletic-looking white man and a short, stocky black woman. They looked ready to deal with whatever they might find as if they were used to running into danger.

I believed the threat in this situation had been largely eliminated.

'What've we got here?' asked the young male officer. He came around the rear end of my car taking care to avoid stepping on some hellebores just coming into bloom. 'Everyone stay calm, please. My name is Constable Hardacre, this is Constable Woods,' he indicated his colleague.

John Ramsey spoke before I could. 'I want this woman charged with assault and the dog terminated.' He shot daggers from his eyes and glared at me the whole time.

'Oooh, doggy!' said the female officer, her eyes going wide when she saw Buster.

John moved toward the edge of the car, looking to see if he could get down now. Buster was distracted by the woman cooing at him. 'I've been stuck on top of my car for fifteen minutes waiting for someone who isn't insane to get here.'

'What a lovely doggy woggy, yes!' Constable Woods cooed, bending over. Buster was a sucker for anyone that would baby talk him, padding in her direction with his back end wagging so hard he almost fell over.

Until John attempted to step down from his car that is.

'Whoa!' exclaimed both police officers as Buster swung through ninety degrees, darted forward, and headbutted a tyre.

John scrambled to get his leading leg out of the way in time. Managing to get back to safety on the bonnet only to almost slide off when the whole car rocked from Buster's impact.

Buster shook his head. '*That one hurt*,' he whined.

Reassessing the danger, Constable Hardacre asked, 'Can you put your dog on his lead, madam?'

Now that the police were here, John Ramsey's innocence or otherwise was their problem, not mine. I called to Buster. 'Come here, boy.'

He licked his face, his tongue slobbering out between his exposed canines. '*I think I bruised my nose,*' he complained. He came to me though, wagging his tail still. It had been a fun game apparently.

'I should check on the victim,' I announced to the police officers once Buster was secure.

'Your name, please?' asked PC Hardacre.

'Mrs Felicity Philips,' I replied.

'Is this your domicile?' He had a small tablet in his hand and was making notes.

I shook my head. 'I am just visiting. I am a wedding planner.'

PC Wood's head snapped up to look at me. 'Felicity Philips,' she repeated. 'Hey, weren't you at that Sashatastic wedding that went horribly wrong last weekend?'

'Oh, yeah,' said her partner. 'I heard about that.'

With a sigh, I nodded my head. 'I was there. The bride and groom chose to postpone the ceremony.'

PC Woods snorted a laugh. 'That's not what I heard. We had a bunch of colleagues there and they said Sasha was involved in some kind of murder cover up. They also said her fiancé ran off with an old girlfriend. I'm sorry I missed it; it sounded better than daytime TV.'

She wasn't wrong. There had been a few issues with that particular celebrity wedding. I got paid up front, so the immediate damage was minimal. The longer-term impact was yet to be determined though, and my closest rival, an evil cow of a woman called Primrose Green, was having a field day with the news.

20

Primrose was only too happy to promote her business by using negative press tactics against mine. Mostly what she said wasn't true so imagine the fun she could have when there was genuine gossip to spread.

It was something I would need to address very soon.

John climbed down from his car, swearing and complaining still. He showed the officers a wound on his leg - I have done worse damage shaving mine.

They were asking questions, and insisting John accompany them to the house so they could establish what might have happened.

'I'll need your keys, sir,' said PC Woods, holding out her hand expectantly. 'I need to move your car so we can unblock the lane outside.' She twitched her eyes to me. 'You too, Mrs Philips.'

PC Hardacre held his arms out to his sides to herd John and me inside the house. Over his shoulder, he said, 'Patience, come and find us once you are done.'

She called back that she wouldn't be long just before we heard her revving the Range Rover's engine. John turned around to see what she was doing, his forehead creasing.

'Is she insured to drive my car?' he wanted to know, acting as if it were something precious. I had no such concerns about mine; it's covered in Buster slobber most of the time.

John was also laying it on thick with his leg wound, limping in an exaggerated way as he hobbled toward the house.

I hurried my steps, getting to the house first because I wanted to hear about Derek's condition. It was quite the tumble from the upper floor of the house, and he didn't move in the time that I was outside with him.

'I need to sit down,' complained John. 'That rabid dog bit me.'

'Buster is not rabid!' I snapped, insulted by the suggestion. I looked down to find Buster had slobbery foam around his chops. 'He's just a bit dribbly,' I tried to defend him. 'If you hadn't shoved Derek off his balcony, none of this would have happened.'

John's face turned instantly red as he raged, 'I didn't push him!'

'You can sit there, sir,' PC Hardacre pointed to an armchair. We were going through their kitchen at the back of the house. Ahead of us, the patio doors were ajar, cool air drifting in and along with it the voices from outside.

A quick glance was all it took to confirm Derek was still unconscious. A paramedic was heading back toward the house, jogging while awkwardly holding onto the various paraphernalia attached to her uniform.

'I need the backboard from the ambulance,' she announced, cruising into the room but pausing to speak with PC Hardacre. 'Is the lane clear now?'

PC Woods came into the kitchen just as the paramedic asked the question.

'It sure is. I need you to move the ambulance so I can get my squad car off the road. There is a tractor already waiting.'

PC Hardacre started toward the front of the house. 'I'll shift it, Patience. You already put a dent in it this week.'

'That wasn't my fault,' she called after him. She did not, however, attempt to stop him. Instead, she moved around the kitchen. 'Anyone for tea?'

I guess police officers are used to going into other people's houses and helping themselves. They must have to deliver notice of death or let people know their loved one has been arrested or been in an accident. Such news might then demand liquid refreshment – everything is better with a cup of tea.

I wasn't entirely convinced most of her colleagues would also help themselves to the chocolate digestives when they found them, but PC Woods put away three while the kettle boiled.

The paramedic came back through the house with what looked like a stripped-down hospital bed on wheels. On it was what I recognised from TV shows as a backboard – a device onto which a casualty could be strapped so they were immobile in transit.

'How is he?' I wanted to know.

I got a noncommittal mumble in reply which I took to be a bad thing.

With PC Hardacre also returning, the two officers got down to the task of finding out what had happened. It felt like a slow response – like they should have got to it sooner, but I guess everyone was calm and they were focused on keeping it that way.

John Ramsey explained who he was and why he was at the house, details I already knew. Then he was quite honest about his verbal altercation with Derek earlier.

'I stormed from the house,' he admitted. 'I got in my car and I went for a long drive. I was very angry.' To me it sounded like a dangerous emotion to admit but he did so willingly.

'Where did you go?' asked PC Hardacre, taking notes again.

'Allhallows,' John replied with a shrug. 'It was just somewhere to go. I went down onto the beach and skimmed stones like I used to when I was a kid. That's our logo, you know.' He produced a business card. On it was a black and white image of a child skimming stones across a pond.

PC Hardacre recapped. 'So you left here angry and skimmed stones. Then what?'

'I calmed down while I was on the beach. I figured I needed to come back to speak with Derek again. I had gotten angry earlier and I shouted at him. We've been friends for fifty years and never exchanged a cross word. I was going to apologise and also try to talk some sense into him. He needs to hand over his role as CEO of the firm and he needs to do it now.'

There was that sense of urgency again. It was as if John felt tomorrow would be too late. Also, why did he want it to go to Tarquin? Wouldn't John, with all his experience, be the better man to take the helm?

PC Woods skipped to the good bit. 'How did he come to fall from the balcony?' There was no inflection in her voice to suggest it was an accusation.

As if sensing he might be better off saying nothing, he said, 'I'm not saying another thing without a lawyer present.'

Neither officer looked surprised.

Woods' radio squawked as a message came over it – more officers had arrived outside. It was a good thing too, because in the next second, the patio doors swung outward to reveal Joanne and Tamara Bleakwith coming in.

Joanne went nuts!

'How dare you come back into this house!' she shrieked at John.

He recoiled, jerking away from her even though he remained sitting. She was coming across the kitchen, advancing with menacing steps. It was fortunate that PC Hardacre was there to get in her way, for I fear she may have physically attacked him otherwise.

PC Woods went to answer the door, letting her colleagues in. A moment later, I heard a voice I knew asking questions. I groaned inwardly and closed my eyes.

'Ah, Mrs Philips,' said the voice as it entered the kitchen, and I opened my eyes while wishing the sight before me would turn out to be a bad dream.

'Hello, Chief Inspector,' I replied. I first met Chief Inspector Quinn last weekend at Loxton Hall. Standing a mite over six feet tall, he was clean-shaven and pasty white. His neatly trimmed hair was as perfectly turned out as his uniform and he looked the sort who ran every morning before work to ensure he was fit and healthy.

He might be a good police officer, but he wasn't a particularly nice person and didn't care one bit if that was what people thought. He acted as if he knew best about everything and believed his authority should be unquestioned. Patricia Fisher made him look like a fool and I had gotten to see it.

He didn't like that one bit.

Joanne was still seething, her eyes boring holes into her husband's business partner's head. However, the paramedics, with her husband loaded on their wheeled gurney, needed to come through the kitchen and that meant she had to move.

'Mr Bleakwith's condition?' asked the chief inspector of the two paramedics.

It was the female of the pair who answered. 'Stable, but unconscious. Mr Bleakwith needs urgent medical treatment but there are no life-threatening injuries that we can find. The backboard is just a precaution until the hospital can complete further scans of his spine. We really need to get moving.'

Wasting no further energy on words, the paramedics set off for the front door, Tamara going with them.

'Are you coming, mum?' she called from the kitchen door.

Joanne still had her eyes locked on John Ramsey. 'I need to get my keys and purse,' she replied without looking Tamara's way. As if noticing the police officers for the first time she said, 'he pushed my husband. I saw him do it. I will testify to it.'

John looked mortified with shock. 'But you didn't see me, Joanne. You were in the living room.'

Chief Inspector Quinn narrowed his eyes. 'You made sure of that, did you?'

'What? No! I ...' John Ramsey realised how close to a confession his previous sentence came.

With a nod toward PC Hardacre, the chief inspector said, 'John Ramsey I am placing you under arrest for the crime of attempted murder ...' he rattled off the standard words of arrest; words I felt sure he must have spoken hundreds of times.

John looked utterly gobsmacked. He was invited to stand, the cuffs going on no sooner than he was on his feet. A nod from the chief inspector and PC Hardacre led John from the room in silence.

I couldn't say why, but seeing John being led away made me smile. 'Good riddance,' I muttered loud enough for him to hear. When he turned his head, I added, 'This is what you get for being a bully all your life.'

'Stop,' commanded Quinn. I couldn't tell who the instruction was aimed at. Was it me? Or his officers? Or everyone? Whoever it was, the chief inspector's next words were aimed at me. 'You know the accused?'

I curled my lip slightly to show how unhappy I was about it. 'We went to school together.'

'You are not friends?' Chief Inspector Quinn sounded surprised.

I shook my head. 'No, we are not. Even if we had been, I would happily testify that he just attempted to kill Derek. I heard the scream and saw him running from the house.'

'I didn't push him,' John insisted again. He was sticking to his story.

I didn't bother to argue.

Chief Inspector Quinn looked at Hardacre. 'Has Mrs Philips given a statement yet?'

'Not as such, sir,' admitted PC Hardacre. 'We were not expecting anyone else to get here this quickly.'

'Efficient as always, Hardacre,' replied the chief inspector snidely.

I thought the first two officers to arrive handled the situation remarkably well.

Joanne reappeared with her coat and handbag; she and Tamara were going to the hospital with Derek. However, the chief inspector wasn't leaving. 'I'm afraid Mrs Bleakwith that since you have accused a man of attempted murder, it will be necessary for my officers to inspect the house and the location where the alleged assault took place. I'm afraid I must insist that either you or your daughter remain here with us.'

Joanne flapped her lips a couple of times, looking like a fish as she tried to form a response. In the end she managed to say, 'But I have to go with Derek.'

Tamara came to her rescue. 'It's okay, mum. I'll stay.'

They exchanged a brief hug and a few words before Joanne went for the front door and Tamara took off her coat.

Chief Inspector Quinn called after her, 'I will need a statement from you still, Mrs Bleakwith. One of my officers will accompany you to the hospital.'

Joanne hurried away, a nod from the chief inspector sending a constable after her.

PC Hardacre followed her out, leading John Ramsey with PC Woods bringing up the rear.

I was given the chance to provide my statement there and then. In it I listed the events in chronological order. The overheard argument, John's angry departure and subsequent return more than an hour later, the scream and then John's flight from the house. I held back from adding any opinion, I doubted it would be helpful, but I did ask if I had done the right thing by blocking his exit with my car and then using Buster to corner the suspect like a cat up a tree.

John was already on his way to the station, probably Maidstone, I guessed.

PC Woods, recording my statement, said, 'It was very brave of you to stop him leaving like that. I wish we had more citizens willing to get involved.'

'No,' argued Chief Inspector Quinn. 'We do not want that at all, Woods. Well-meaning civilians always cause more trouble than they prevent and create more problems than they solve. Police work is to be left to the police, Mrs Philips. I applaud your bravery, but just like last weekend, I must remind you that what you should have done was stay out of the way and swiftly placed a call to the authorities. We are equipped and trained to deal with such situations. What would you have done if he had been armed?'

'Screamed and run away,' I replied snippily. 'I can run very fast.'

I got a raised eyebrow and an assessing look in return. 'I dare say you can. Nevertheless, I do not condone your actions.' His assessing look turned curious, worry pinching his eyes to narrow them. 'You won't be calling Mrs Fisher, will you, Mrs Philips?' he asked cagily. He tried to make the question sound causal and failed miserably to fool me that it was.

However, for a second, I couldn't work out why he was asking me about my old acquaintance, Patricia Fisher. I hadn't seen her in years until last weekend. A heart beat later the reason for his question dawned on me like someone turning on a lightbulb – he was afraid I might involve the local sleuth who upstaged him so completely last weekend at Loxton Hall. As a professional crime-buster, it must pain him to have someone swoop in to solve a case when the answer eluded him.

Giving him my full attention, I asked, 'You think she might take an interest in this case?'

Blustering, he replied, 'I cannot imagine why she would.'

His behaviour made me laugh, and it also made me act very much out of character for I said, 'I cannot imagine either. I'm sure she has something far more complex to investigate. Figuring out why John pushed Derek over the balcony railing and proving it was him would be no challenge at all for her.' I waited for the chief inspector to cast his gaze my way once more, before adding. 'I think I'll just solve this one myself.'

PC Woods snorted, a laugh escaping her lips at my direct challenge. I'd basically thrown down the gauntlet or slapped the chief inspector across the face with it – pick your metaphor. The young police officer hid her face, turning so her boss couldn't see her and walking a few paces away as her shoulders shook.

I cannot for the life of me tell you why I thought to make such a declaration, but there it was, out in the open and there was no way to hide from it now.

The Boutique

Driving to Rochester, I continued to wonder why my mouth had chosen to run away with itself.

'What on Earth were you thinking, Felicity?' I asked myself, speaking aloud in the confines of my convertible Mercedes SL sports car. 'What, you're going to swap your lucrative career as a wedding planner to be a sleuth just because Patricia Fisher made it look not only easy but very cool?'

I was mad at myself. The chief inspector chose to laugh in my face, undoubtedly because he saw my ridiculous statement for what it was. Now I had to find a way to back down without losing any more face.

From the passenger seat where he was as securely strapped in as one can a sixty-pound furry sack of playdough, Buster said, '*I think this is the coolest thing you have ever decided to do. I can be your sidekick.*'

'I don't need a sidekick, thank you, Buster.'

'*Sure you do. All great crime fighters have one. Just look at The Green Hornet, he had Kato. Now there was a cool sidekick.*'

'Where did you see *The Green Hornet*?' I wanted to know.

Buster gave me the canine equivalent of a shrug. '*I was chewing that thingy you keep out of my reach.*'

'The TV remote?' I guessed.

'*Yeah, that. Well, the TV came on as it usually does if I chew it for long enough and there was this cool black and white show.*'

I rolled my eyes. 'Buster you think all shows are black and white.'

'*That's because they are,*' he argued. '*Anyway, that's the kind of sidekick I want to be. Just like Kato, not some comedy punchbag there to make the hero look good.*'

'I am not a crime fighter. I will not be investigating what happened to Derek.'

Buster turned his head and eyes to look up at me. '*Please? I need some excitement. Look at my body. Do you think this body was made for sitting around listening to weddings being planned*?' He looked like a baked potato with tusks and a tail. '*I was built for stopping bad guys.*' He growled and swiped at the air with a paw.

I patted his head. 'Sorry, Buster, Felicity is a wedding planner.'

I got grumpy noises from him for the next ten minutes which was how long it took to get to Rochester.

I have a small boutique just off Rochester High Street. It's convenient for my home in Twydhurst, just the other side of the river and I get a lot of passing traffic. Also, the history of the area, the high price of rent, and the delightful ambience the castle, cathedral, and Dickensian architecture bring, all made it not only a great place to work, but also somewhere clients wish to visit.

I could slash my rent by ninety percent if I moved to one of the industrial estates – there were several less than half a mile from my office – but the rich and the famous would drive by me without ever thinking to stop.

The office boasts two bowed windows, one either side of the door. Each is divided into sixteen small panes that give the boutique and displays in the windows a wonderful old feel. They don't make shops like this now. The period features make the front façade elegant in a way that could not be reproduced using modern materials. The building is over three hundred years old.

I loved all the little features of the place and how well preserved many of them were. Upstairs, there is a fireplace in one of the back bedrooms where children had scratched their names into the brickwork. Hidden inside the flue, I might never have noticed them if the estate agent hadn't pointed it out to me. Someone – a former tenant – had traced the history of the building back to discover the names belonged to three children living in the house in the 1860s. They would all be long dead now, but their descendants might live in the area still and there was something deeply romantic about the building still holding their names.

I found Justin Cutler at his desk. Justin is in his forties and married with two children. Lean and average height, he also has average looks but wears fabulous suits that make him stand out. He is also one of those people who is brimming with natural confidence. In front of people being the centre of attention is his natural habitat. It made him a very good master of ceremonies. Today his shirt was a dusty shade of pink and his suit was bright white with a thin purple pinstripe. His shoes were white too with purple laces.

Not for the first time, I found myself wondering where he shopped.

Looking up over the top of his reading glasses to see who was coming in – most visitors were by appointment – he said, 'Oh, hi, Felicity. I see you got away at last. What happened?'

When I called him earlier to cancel our lunch meeting, I gave him only a cursory explanation. Now he got the full run down.

Mindy, my niece and assistant (in that order) came in from a back room where she had been sorting through marketing materials. Now free of his lead, Buster scampered across the room to see her.

'Is this about the Bleakwiths?' she asked. 'Justin said something happened and the police were involved.'

Mindy is as curious as every other teenager I have ever met, which is to say not even slightly interested unless it is something that interests her. I could try to explain marketing techniques and the use of colour for advertising until I was blue in the face; none of it would sink in. However, if I mention the name of a celebrity who might come by the boutique, she is all ears.

Someone getting pushed off a balcony also fell into the category of worth hearing about. At nineteen, Mindy has that almost perfect body most of us remember having. She is tall at nearly five feet ten inches, and moves with a sinuous, almost feral, quality. She wears a lot of black, tight-fitting clothing designed to move with her body and is a black belt third dan in karate, I recently learned. Her hair is pink, undercut with jet black to give an effect which I wouldn't want for myself, yet must accept suits her. Today, she had on office wear – a grey pencil skirt and a silk blouse. The heels were colour matched to the blouse. I give her an allowance for clothing because in this game we need to look the part.

I backtracked a little going over the events of Derek's house again so she could hear. I ended by admitting my foolish challenge to the chief inspector.

'Oh, cool!' cheered Mindy. 'I can be your sidekick!'

I sniggered. 'Buster already claimed that job.'

I got an odd look from both Justin and my niece and worried I was going to have to laugh it off as if it were just my little joke. I told you earlier I have a habit of forgetting no one else knows about my special ability.

Justin said, 'Seriously though, you're not going to investigate, are you?'

'Goodness, no,' I found myself laughing at the idea even though I had to acknowledge I rather fancied wiping the smile from the chief inspector's face. 'No, I have far too much to do already.' I really did. Pushing silly thoughts of searching for clues from my mind, I took out my tablet. 'I have notes from today's meeting with the Bleakwiths.' I got down to business, calling Mindy across to my desk. If I was going to treat her as a serious assistant and teach her the ropes, she needed to start learning how to manage people.

That could start with Tamara's very exacting pink gerbera demands. When Mindy left the boutique ten minutes later with Buster leading the way, she was heading for Carson's florist in the High Street. They were another firm with which I had a great relationship. They made sure my boutique was always stocked with a fresh bouquet in the window and I gave them a lot of business. With Mindy planning to collect coffee on the way back, I turned my attention to the wedding we had set for next weekend.

At my end of the market, I am not trying to cram in a wedding every weekend; I select only the most prominent or most interesting clients. However, that can mean several in a single month if that is the way they fall and that was what I had now.

After the debacle of the Howard-Box wedding last weekend, we needed to focus on the next event. In exactly eight days' time, on Friday next week, we were all travelling to Raven Island off the south coast of Kent. In Raven's Bluff, the palatial folly built there, we were to be witness to the marriage of Anton Harker, a popular TV host, and Geoffrey Banks, a soap opera star. They had money and fame which made them a great catch for Philips' Wedding Plans.

Justin joined me and we started to plot the detail of how we would meet the groom and groom's needs. There was much to plan but where any other day I would be completely focused on what I was doing, today I found myself distracted by thoughts of Derek Bleakwith and John Ramsey.

It was only when Mindy returned with the coffee and I took a few moments to think about what I needed to do over the weekend, that I remembered something that made my heart skip a beat in fright.

The fact that I had a date tonight was scary enough; I haven't been on a date since my husband, Archie, died a little more than three years ago and, to be honest, I don't think nights out with your spouse really count. In which case, I hadn't been out on a date in over three decades.

There was a certain terror that went with meeting Vince Slater for dinner and I knew what it was that scared me. It wasn't that he had shown interest in me right from the moment we met, or that I was going on this date because I found myself tricked into agreeing to it – Patricia Fisher had a lot to answer for – but more that Vince awakened in me a sense of hope.

At fifty-five, I was consciously refusing to acknowledge that I was throwing myself into my work because I just didn't have that much else going on in my life. I didn't need a man. At least I didn't want to need a man and fervently believed I could live the rest of my life alone. However, I also believed Archie would be sad to know I had so little waiting for me at home each night.

So Vince showed up with his heroic actions, saving my life while getting injured and being ever so brave about it. He had a pirate's smile, one which any woman could tell was bad news but liked to look at anyway. He was also handsome, strong, and courageous. He looked after himself, had his own money ... the list of positive attributes was probably quite a long one if I got to think about it. However, and this is a pretty big however, I wasn't looking for a relationship. The idea that I might one day share my bed with another man quite frankly terrified me.

Nevertheless, I was going out for dinner with him tonight. It was just dinner. I would drive and maybe have one glass of red wine. He was paying, and I picked an expensive restaurant that most people cannot get into but ... well, I have a book of contacts and the ability to leverage a relationship when required. Not that I was doing anything the restaurant owner was unhappy with, I like to think all my professional relationships are mutually beneficial. I recommend those businesses whose attributes and standards are most aligned with my own. In so doing I ensure my customers will talk about every element of their interaction with me in a positive tone.

Mindy had a date tonight as well, though at nineteen her dates were a wholly different beast to mine. She left the boutique just a few minutes after five which was quite late enough. I stayed on another twenty minutes to finish up the notes from the Bleakwith meeting. Sitting at my desk in the pool of light thrown by the antique lamps I vastly preferred to the overhead strip lighting, I thought some more about what happened to Derek.

What had I actually seen today? Looking back at the images in my head, John Ramsey was either a good actor or he really hadn't pushed Derek over the balcony. I heard him when he spoke and saw his face – he looked innocent to me. Yet the chief inspector had him arrested on the spot; the testimony of the victim's wife sufficient to convince him of John's guilt.

Coming back to the here and now with a jolt, I realised ten minutes had passed while I stared at the inside of my own head. It was Buster who disturbed my train of thought as he got up to inform me his stomach was rumbling. Had he not done so, I might have sat there for hours.

Amber, my pedigree ragdoll cat, was at home and would also want dinner. It was time to go.

My house is a cottage on the other side of the River Medway. The ancient bridge spanning the wide swathe of dirty brown water is often clogged when I leave the boutique, but not so today, and I made the journey in just under fifteen minutes.

Just outside of Strood which sits on the hill on the far side of the Medway valley, the small village of Twydhurst has a pub and a corner shop with a post office inside and very little of anything else unless you count the church. I have lived there for twelve years, ever since the cottage I fell in love with as a child came up for sale.

I had a battle to buy it and paid over the odds to secure it because the other buyer foolishly admitted a desire to bulldoze it. His plan was to build a modern, six-double-bedroom property on the footprint of the original single-story house. I have never once regretted my decision.

Since moving in I have decorated and added a modern kitchen because the old lady who inhabited before me was still using standalone appliances and a cooker from the nineteenth century. A modern bathroom was required as well, but otherwise, the delightful cottage was untouched. It was small, but it had been big enough for Archie and me.

Amber was sitting on the carpet in the hallway twitching her tail at me in a display of bored annoyance. '*It's about time,*' she muttered, making sure I saw how disappointed she was before turning around to saunter off with her tail held high.

'Yes, Amber, I'm sure you are not actually starving,' I pointed out, shedding my coat and bending to take off my boots by the door.

'*My stomach is empty enough that it woke me from my nap, Felicity,*' she mewled in disgust. '*That means I am operating on reduced sleep and will now have to squeeze in an extra nap before my main sleep tonight.*' What a terrible dilemma. '*I see you brought the dog home with you again,*' she complained as she sashayed out of sight and into the kitchen.

I swung my hand to grab Buster's collar, but he was already running, his tiny legs shooting him along the hallway carpet. He and Amber had never seen eye to eye, each of them doing their best to aggravate the other at every opportunity. Amber claimed the house as her own, constantly seeking ways to get the awful dog smell out of it. Buster believed the house was his and would mark Amber's bed if he got the chance.

I kept her bed on the counter in the kitchen.

Hopping, as I tried to get the stupid zip on my left boot to move, I gave up and hobbled after my pets with one boot on and the other off. Buster was barking his death threats and must have got close enough to Amber to scare her because she made that horrible hissing rowling noise cats manage to create. Hobbling through the kitchen door, I got to hear something smash.

Shards of white china covered the stone tile of the kitchen floor. It was the lid from my Aunt Ida's butter dish and as I tried to yell, 'No!' Amber flicked the base of the butter dish off the counter too.

Buster was on his hind legs, standing up to bark at the cat though he knew he was several inches too short to ever get to her.

'*Come here, cat! I'll make mincemeat of you!*' Buster threatened.

Amber looked over the side and swatted his nose the next time he tried to jump at her. '*There's a good doggy. Keep acting predictably for me. Look Buster, there's butter on the floor.*'

Momentarily distracted, Buster glanced, saw the butter, and swooped on it. Sure, he wanted to kill the cat, but food was food. Unfortunately, he was dumb enough to eat the shards of broken china too. He would most likely think they were put there deliberately to add some extra texture and crunch.

I shooed him back, finally getting hold of his collar so I could drag him from the room.

'*But the butter!*' he barked. '*I'll clean it up for you.*'

With a final shove, I got him into the hallway and shut the door.

Amber licked a paw with feigned nonchalance. '*Isn't it so much nicer with him anywhere but where we are?*' she commented lazily.

I blew out a frustrated sigh. 'No, Amber. I like Buster living here. You and I have this conversation most days.' From the cupboard in the corner, I took out a dustpan and brush along with some anti-grease spray and got onto my hands and knees.

'*Do we?*' asked Amber, still sounding bored. '*I hardly remember. Any conversation about the dog isn't worth remembering. Unless you wanted to talk about taking him to the vets, of course. I would listen to that conversation with interest. I hear they do a very cost sensitive service in both euthanasia and castration. I would even come with you to help you through any emotional nonsense you might feel.*'

From the carpet tile, I looked up to meet Amber's radiant sapphire eyes. 'Emotional nonsense?'

She twitched her tail and licked her paw again, using it to wipe around her left ear. '*Yes. You know how you humans get – all silly and teary eyed just because the dog's carcass went in the bin.*'

'That's horrible,' I gasped, shocked that she would talk about Buster in such terms.

Amber paused her grooming to look down at me. *'Only for the dog,'* she pointed out as if I might have missed a vital point. *'You and I would be able to continue our lives and think how much happier I would be. That's got to be worth the cost of the visit, surely.'*

Becoming vexed, I got off my knees, scooped Amber and took her to the kitchen door.

'You need to go outside and think about how awful I would feel if anything happened to either one of you.' I plopped her unceremoniously on the step outside and closed the door.

'But you would have me to comfort you,' Amber explained, strolling back in through the kitty door as if nothing had happened.

I picked her up again, this time moving fast before she tried to escape me, shot the lock on the kitty door, and placed her back on the step outside.

With a wagging finger, I said, 'Buster is your brother, and you should be nicer to him.'

I got a raised eyebrow. *'Brother? I think I just threw up in my mouth.'*

I shut the door and went back to the mess of Aunt Ida's butter dish.

Buster was pawing at the internal kitchen door, Amber was meowing loudly at the door to the garden, and I felt like pouring a large glass of wine.

So I did. There is generally a bottle of something crisp, white, and overpriced in my fridge. My nearest supermarket is a Waitrose – the highest of the high end of regular supermarkets – so I always get the best of whatever I have on my shopping list, but one must pay the mark up for it.

Savouring a moment of peace as the chilled wine slipped over my tastebuds, I blocked out the sound of my pets. Moment over, I got on with getting them fed.

Amber eats on the kitchen counter, Buster on the floor. Any other combination has proven to be fatally flawed.

Feeling content, which you can translate to hoping fervently, that they would fill their bellies and retreat to separate corners of the house to sleep, I went upstairs to shower and change.

My table at the Wild Oak in Aylesford was reserved for eight o'clock, a time I felt was neither early nor late. I hadn't eaten at the restaurant since before Archie died though I remembered their excellent steaks well.

I'm sure most women would shave their legs before going on a date. I did not for I was quite certain (thank you) that Vince would not get to see them. It's not like I have hairy legs like a rugby player after all. In the same vein, I threw on the first items of underwear my hand fell upon.

This was a functional event where two people were going to eat dinner and have a conversation. It was nothing more than that. A rumble of emptiness from my belly convinced me to eat a cheese cracker. It went well with the last of the wine in my glass and would have to keep me going for a while because even though our table was booked for half an hour from now, I knew it would be most of another thirty minutes after that before I got to eat anything.

Perhaps some olives to nibble at the table would suffice.

Pausing at the door to my living room, I raised my voice to address Amber and Buster. 'Can I count on you to stay out of each other's way while I am out?' I asked, a hint of warning in my tone.

Amber lifted her head and opened one eye. '*Out? Where are you going?*'

'*She's mating,*' said Buster.

'I am not!' I spluttered.

Buster, spread across the rug by the radiator like a melted chocolate bar, rolled over to meet my eyes. '*You're going out to meet a man, right?*'

'Yes, but.'

'*Sounds like mating to me,*' said Amber, the cat and dog agreeing on something for once.

I was frowning so hard my eyebrows threatened to kiss my cheeks. '*I am not mating. There will be no mating.*'

Buster rolled back over. 'Humans are so weird about mating.'

I started to argue but caught myself before I could stamp my foot in frustration. 'Just make sure the house looks the same as it does now when I get back. I don't want any torn cushions, Buster,' he flipped his head around to shoot me a 'Who me?' expression. 'And I don't want my curtains shredded, Amber.'

Amber didn't even bother to look up, scorning me with her indifference.

With an exasperated breath that this was my life, I snatched up my handbag, checked the contents and left the house. It would take me twenty minutes to get to the restaurant and though I didn't want to go, I wasn't rude enough to arrive late.

Or so I thought.

Orion Printing is one of those places you drive by a thousand times without ever noticing. Until you have a reason to notice it, that is. I knew where the business was, of course, I have been there thousands of times to drop things off or to collect. It is less than a hundred yards from The Wild Oak, but only when I parked my car did I remember they shared the same carpark.

By the river in the small village, the small-scale, yet successful printing business was right there in front of me. It would be more accurate to say the back of it was as I was facing the rear of the building. Ahead of me, in a row that backed against the rear wall of a small line of businesses, several spaces were reserved for employees.

To my surprise and confusion, one of the spaces was taken by a large blue Range Rover. John Ramsey's Range Rover to be exact. I felt certain it was the same one but moved in closer to satisfy my curiosity. The lights in the carpark beat away most of the dark, but behind the rear wall of the buildings, inky black shadows ruled. I needed the torch on my phone to be able to see the scratches Buster left with his claws earlier today.

Was he out of custody already? How had he managed that? I felt sure Joanne's statement would be sufficient to convict.

Peering through the passenger window, I saw a mound of paperwork on the seat. It was loose leaves of paper; lines of numbers that looked like a profit and loss statement or a cashflow report. I had an accountant firm on contract to deal with mine. It was probably something I could do but subcontracting it out gave me more time to work on the business. Basically, I knew more or less that what I was looking at were financial statements but that was about it.

What I noted, when I shone my torch around, was the red circles around some of the figures. Lines came from more than one with exclamation marks at the end. Straining my eyes to see, I was leaning on the car and jumped half out of my skin when the door shifted.

It hadn't been properly closed. Glancing at the popper thingy, I could see the car wasn't locked. My heart rate spiked, not because I was now worried John was nearby, but because I knew what I was going to do if he wasn't.

I stepped back a little, peering around the edge of the car to see if anyone was about. The carpark was empty and silent. I could hear the river gurgling twenty yards away behind the cars. My heart started to hammer in my chest as I went back to the passenger door. The paperwork was right there!

All I had to do was open the door and grab it. I could decipher it later, but anyone could see there was something about it that had spiked John's interest. All the exclamation marks had to mean something. Another squint through the window showed there were notes at the bottom of the page, but they were handwritten and too difficult to read upside down in the dark.

A question surfaced in my head. *What would Patricia do?*

Knowing I absolutely shouldn't, I grabbed the door handle anyway. The door popped open just a fraction as I held it almost closed and looked guiltily about again. Standing on my tippy toes, I still wasn't tall enough to see over John's car, but I couldn't hear anyone approaching, so I opened the door another inch.

The light came on inside, bathing my face in light. Panicking, I yanked the door open far enough to snake my arm inside, grabbed the top few pieces of paper, and pushed it shut again.

My heart was threatening to leave my chest, it was pounding so hard. The pages got stuffed unceremoniously into my handbag just before I stepped back out into the light from the overhead lamps.

There, caught like a thief in a searchlight, I froze to the spot. John Ramsey was twenty yards away and he was looking right at me.

He froze too, but only for a half second. Then he was shouting and angry and coming my way at a run.

'You again! What the devil are you doing here? Are you set to ruin me? Are you in on it? Is this all just because I was horrible to you when we were little?' The torrent of questions seemed likely to never end until they did.

They ended because I panicked and shouted, 'I'll scream if you come any closer!'

The warning was enough to make his advance falter, but it also caused a new question. 'What were you doing by my car?' His voice was calmer – not shouting at least – but there was no mistaking the threat behind his words.

'I wanted to confirm it was yours,' I told him truthfully. 'How come the police let you go?' I asked because the question begged an answer.

'I was released on bail,' he growled through gritted teeth. 'Thanks to you and Joanne, I am in the frame for attempting to kill my oldest friend. He jumped, and whether he dies or not and whether they convict me or not, he will still have jumped.' The rage behind his words made me back away a pace. I will admit I was scared.

I'm a small woman and I was alone in a dark car park with a man who might have already tried to murder one person today. I did not feel like giving him a chance to improve his batting average by getting it right this time.

Seeing me back away another pace, John took a step forward. 'What's the matter, Felicity? Afraid I might hurt you? I don't hurt people!' he thundered. 'Not ever. I didn't push Derek, I tried to stop him. I am not the crook in this equation.'

I felt the muscles of my right eyebrow tug, as it climbed my forehead. 'Who is the crook?'

My question seemed to amuse him, a smile pulling the corner of his mouth. 'Why would I bother telling you? You wouldn't believe me.' He pointed his key fob at the car, and the boot lid slowly opened skyward the next moment. In his hands he held a cardboard box, the kind one might employ to clear out one's desk. Dumping it over the tailgate so it vanished inside the dark boot space, he reached up to grab the boot lid once more.

Then he paused and turned to face me. 'You don't deserve to know the truth, Felicity. You certainly don't deserve to know the truth about me. No one does.' He shifted his stance, turning his body to face me.

I was staring at him, unable to convince my legs to move for fear he was going to chase me and drown me in the river.

His hands clenched into fists, but his feet didn't move, his mouth did. 'It will ruin me, but when I can prove it, I'll expose the truth.'

He could see my fear, I felt sure he could, but if he was thinking about killing me, he changed his mind because he snorted a small laugh at my terror and got in his car. I still hadn't moved when he pulled away, the taillights of his car disappearing from sight when he rounded the first corner.

I was left alone in the car park, my heart still beating away at twice its usual speed and that's when my phone rang.

I almost wet myself.

The shrill noise in the near silence of the carpark made my heart stop and restart. As a result, a wave of nausea and a lightheaded sensation combined to make me believe I might faint. I had to dip my head while looking about for something I might grab to keep myself upright.

A streetlight was the only obvious choice, so I staggered to it, clinging on like a person trapped in a sudden flood that threatened to wash them away. A fumbling hand found my phone.

'Hello,' I stammered breathlessly.

'Felicity?' It was Vince calling me, no doubt wondering where I might have gotten to given that I was now fifteen minutes late for my date. 'Felicity, are you all right?'

I gasped to get a breath in so that I could calm myself and answer without sounding like I'd just narrowly avoided being John Ramsey's second victim.

'I'm fine,' I wheezed, certain I didn't sound it. 'I'll be there in two minutes. I'm in the car park down the road.'

'I'll come to you,' he snapped out as a fast reply and the phone went dead.

He didn't need any more information to find me; there is only one carpark in Aylesford. He was coming to me. An entirely unnecessary gesture since I was completely okay and not in the slightest bit shaken. That was what I was going to tell him anyway.

Cursing myself for being so easily frightened, I forced my legs to obey my commands and started toward the restaurant. I got three paces before the sound of someone running reached my ears. They were coming my way and two seconds later, Vince Slater appeared.

He was wearing a smart, yet casual, jacket and shirt combination but despite his office clothes, he looked almost predatory as he stepped into the carpark looking for me. His expression was intense and dangerous, enough so that it made me question his past. Was he ex special forces or something? Was he a former member of MI5? Catching myself fantasising about him as if I were some lovesick schoolgirl, I waved to make myself visible.

'Over here, Vince. I'm fine. I told you that.'

He jogged across to me, his eyes roving all around as if looking for danger. Slowing to a walk as he closed the last few yards, he scrutinised my face.

'Your pupils are dilated, Felicity. What happened? Did someone attack you?'

'No!' I protested, then accepted that lying to the man was unfair. 'Sort of,' I admitted.

He looked around the carpark again, his eyes hungry for someone his hands could deal with.

'Goodness, will you calm down, Vince. He's gone, okay. He drove off.'

Vince let go a breath he'd been holding, relaxing as he focused his attention solely on me. 'Who was it?' he requested to know.

I had no good reason to tell him anything and I was getting hungry, but I took a minute to tell him about my day, the events at the Bleakwiths' house, and how John Ramsey and I were old enemies.

'He works here?' Vince asked, pointing to the printing business I had just pointed out to him.

'Yes. He co-owns it with Derek Bleakwith, the man he shoved off a balcony today.'

Vince made his eyebrows do a double flip thing, up and down twice in swift succession. Accompanied by a wolf's smile, I knew he was about to do something naughty.

'Perhaps we should have a look at what he has been up to,' he suggested, going around me to head for the rear of the row of businesses.

I was left staring at his back, bewildered for a moment. 'What? Wait, what? What do you mean we should have a look at what he has been up to?'

Vince wasn't waiting for me though, he was already fiddling with the gate that led into the printer's backyard.

'Standard procedure in any investigation, Felicity: look where they don't want you to look, find out what they are trying to keep people from finding out. If he tried to kill his business partner, there has to be a reason. You said he wanted Derek to stand down and to name another employee as his successor, right.

'Tarquin Tremaine. That's his future son-in-law. Derek's daughter works at the firm too. It's a family business.'

'Right.' Vince nodded. 'So John is super urgent to get Tarquin into the role of CEO and that to me sounds highly suspicious. Tarquin must be a puppet or something. John must be planning to control him. Maybe he plans to swindle the Bleakwiths out of their half of the business somehow.'

'That sounds like something John might do.' To be fair, I didn't know John well enough to make such a comment, but he had just scared me, and I wasn't feeling very charitable.

Vince shot another pirate's smile. 'We'll just have a poke around the office.'

The gate popped open and he vanished through it. Once again, I was in the carpark by myself.

My jaw hanging open, I said, 'What?' for the third or fourth time.

Vince's big smiley head poked back out through the hole in the wall. 'Come on, Felicity. It will be fun. They'll hold our table a while longer.'

Vanishing again, I felt compelled to go after him.

'Vince, you can't just break into a property and dig around for clues,' I hissed at the dark shadow in front of me.

'Over here,' I got in reply from my left.

What I took to be Vince was, in fact, an old tarpaulin over some logs. The old buildings would still have real fireplaces inside, but it was a surprise that people might still employ them.

Following his voice in the dark, I arrived as he got the rear door open.

'How did you even do that?' I wanted to know. 'No, forget I asked. Please close the door and come away. No good will come of this. We'll get caught and go to jail,' I was about ready to grab him and insist he take me for dinner. My heart was pounding again. Not like it had been arguing with John, but thumping in my chest, nevertheless.

Vince reached back to grab my hand. 'Look, this place isn't alarmed,' he paused in what he was about to say to add, 'If you are about to ask me

54

how I know, the answer is there are no contacts on the door. If you are going to ask me how I know that then we are going to waste a lot of time. Just trust me on the alarm thing, okay? The police or a security firm will not rush here to find out what is going on so now that we are inside, we can take at least a few minutes to check out the computers and see what we find. You said he is guilty of attempted murder, right?'

'Yes,' I replied slowly because I knew he was going to use it to fuel his next line of reasoning.

'So let's find out why. Maybe this will save your friend's business and when he wakes up, assuming he does because ol' Vince likes to think positive, you can be the one who solved the case, caught the killer, and saved the day.'

He ought to have been a politician with the way he was able to spin things. However, he couldn't hide that we had just performed a very illegal breaking and entering.

'What if someone comes? What if John Ramsey realises he's forgotten something and comes back for it?' I asked, planning to use his answer to make him leave with me.

'Good point,' he replied, pursing his lips, and scratching the back of his head. 'Yes, I hadn't thought of that.' I was about to go back out the door when he added. 'Tell you what; you stay here. If someone comes, you fight them. I'll look for evidence.'

As my eyes flared, he planted a kiss on my lips and vanished into the darkness of the building's interior. I swear his cheeky grin lingered in my vision like the Cheshire Cat's.

'Vince!' I hissed into the darkness. 'Vince!'

I got no answer back, the horrible rogue no doubt thinking himself clever to leave me hanging in the doorway.

Trying to convince myself I should get back in my car and go home, I soon changed my mind when his voice drifted out of the dark. 'I found something.'

Chocolate Biscuits

Cursing myself, I pushed on into the building, carefully closing the door behind me. From the back door of the business, a central hallway linked storerooms and rooms filled with printers to the display area at the front of the business. That area had been set aside for the firm to show off what they could do for potential clients. A pool of light coming from a door led me to Vince. He was in a side office.

'What did you find?' I asked, my pulse racing that he might have already unearthed a big clue.

Mumbling because his mouth was full, he held something up toward me. 'Chocolate biscuits. They're the good ones too.'

'That's what you found?' I gasped, my jaw dropping open again. 'You tricked me in here because you found chocolate biscuits!'

Sounding hurt, his features illuminated only by the light from the computer screen, Vince said, 'I think *tricked* is a bit harsh. I said I found something, and I did. Just because it's not the identity of the third gunman on the grassy knoll ...'

I wanted to slap the offered biscuits away, but my stomach groaned loudly in the dark, making Vince chuckle.

'They have chewy caramel bits in,' he teased.

I snatched the packet and bit into one. He was right; they were good.

'What are you looking for?' I asked him. He was sitting behind a desk and playing with a computer. 'How did you even get into that? Isn't it password protected?'

His eyes never left the screen, but he lifted his left hand, holding up a Post-It note on which an alpha-numeric code was written.

'This was stuck to the bottom of the monitor. To answer your first question, I am looking for what is on this computer. There's way too much to analyse sitting here, so I'm going to copy it to look through later. I have a kid on my payroll who loves this stuff.'

A thumb drive appeared in his hand. I guess when you are a snoopy private eye type person who carries magic tools for breaking into places even when out on a date, a data drive is the kind of thing you have in your pocket just in case there are computer files to steal.

'Isn't all this illegal?' I wanted to know.

'Oh, goodness, yes. Very. We should get out of here and go for dinner.' They were the first words he'd said that made any sense and I was ready to second the vote when my blood froze.

Someone had just put a key in the front door.

I opened my mouth to draw in a horrified gasp and then let out a little squeak as a hand clamped over my face and shut off the supply of air going in.

'Shhh,' whispered Vince, his mouth next to my right ear and so quiet it would not be heard by anyone but me. We had not turned on the light in the office and reaching back to the computer, Vince flicked off the monitor too.

There was light coming in from the street through the floor to ceiling glass windows that fronted the property. Enough to see by and what we were seeing was a shadow.

'We need to move!' hissed Vince, grabbing my hand and dragging me to the office door. The sense of urgency in his voice made my feet move without me telling them to.

At the edge of the frame, he flattened himself, peered around it, and ducked back inside. He swore under his breath and leaned in close to me.

'We're trapped. We need to hide.'

My heart felt like it had been running at maximum speed for the last half an hour. Doing some mental math, I figured it probably had. Well, it wasn't slowing down any time soon because the shadow was coming our way and Vince was pulling me by the hand again.

In the corner of the office we were in, what I took to be a space to the side of a cabinet turned out to be an alcove created when the new office was squeezed in between the original oak columns. Vince ducked inside, pulling me after him and pulling me tight into his body so we both fit.

I pushed away from him, still smarting from the cheeky kiss he stole and very much not wanting to find myself pressed up against him.

Yet again, he clamped his hand over my mouth and wrapped his other arm around my torso to keep me from moving. He'd forgotten about my legs though. They were free to move and as instinct took over, I drove my right knee upwards.

It connected with something soft just as the light came on. Vince choked out a breath and sucked in a gasp of air. To prove a point, I clamped my hands over his mouth and cocked an eyebrow at him.

We were completely invisible in the alcove but would still have to stay quiet and hope whoever had come in wasn't planning to stay long.

'Right,' said a man's voice – a young man, if I was any judge, 'time to erase the evidence.'

Erase the evidence? I heard the words and forgot about my racing heart for a moment as my curiosity took over. What evidence was he erasing? What was it evidence of?

Vince and I were as quiet as quiet could be. I was pressed tight up against him, his heat radiating into me and his aftershave tickling my nose. It was making me very uncomfortable but there was no way to escape yet.

The young man continued chattering to himself. 'Almost done. Nothing left to trace anything back to me.'

I was so desperate to stick my head out to see who it was. Why hadn't I set my phone to record and popped it on a shelf? We could have had this all on video!

'There. All done,' the young man said, and we heard the sound of the chair moving across the carpet and then the pneumatic springs in the legs resetting the chair to its usual height as the man stood up.

My stomach grumbled again, and it was sooo loud. If Vince and I hadn't already been motionless, we would have frozen like statues. Instead, I held my breath and tried to convince my heart to stop beating because the young man had also stopped moving.

He'd heard me.

The blood began to pound in my ears as I refused to draw my next breath. Any second now a hand was going to grab me from behind and we were going to be caught. Goodness knows how many different things we could be charged with.

When the young man laughed, I spasmed in fright, but he said, 'You're getting jumpy.' The sound of his footsteps retreating, accompanied by a rueful chuckle came just as the demand for oxygen reached critical point. I sucked in a deep breath barely able to believe we hadn't been caught.

Vince, however, was on the move. He didn't say anything, but I knew he was trying to get to the office door to get a look at the young man. I had to admit I was desperate to identify him too.

I went after Vince, who was walking funny I noted guiltily, and stopped right on his shoulder as once again he sidled up to the frame of the office door.

The young man, whoever he was, was locking up again. When he rattled the door to make sure it was secure, Vince peeked around the frame and then took a step out into the corridor beyond. Terrified that we might still get caught, our curiosity denying us the clean escape we seemed to have won, I went too.

I needed to see who was burying evidence even though I had no idea what might be going on.

All I could see was an outline. A tall, lean young man, going up the hill. He was there for less than a second and then he was past the window and gone.

'Well, that was fun,' said Vince. 'Shall we get some dinner now?'

Dinner Interruption

I slapped his arm as hard as I could. It had much the same effect as a fly headbutting a car and just made him laugh.

'Vince Slater you almost gave me a heart attack. How on Earth am I breaking into buildings and nearly getting caught by the people who work there? I'm a respectable wedding planner I'll have you know. Getting arrested is not part of my plan.' The plan being to get the job of organising the next royal wedding.

'Stop loitering inside then,' he chuckled, heading for the back door. 'Honestly, woman. Anyone would think you wanted to get caught.'

I felt my lip curl as a retort came to my lips, but I bit it down and followed him back the way we came in. I never once thought about throwing a four-hole punch at his head and you can't prove I did.

As predicted, The Wild Oak had kept our table open though that was mostly due to Vince having some of his things still on it. Keys, reading glasses for the menu and what looked like a past-its-best whisky on the rocks were arranged on one side of the table. The doorman took my coat and the Maître D arrived to escort us through the restaurant.

My heart finally came back to its normal rhythm only once I had been sitting for five minutes and could distract myself with mundanity like the menu. I would never admit it, least of all to the rogue sitting opposite me, but the last hour had been among the most exciting of my life.

The chocolate biscuit had done little to quell my rising hunger though in all the excitement I'd forgotten just how famished I was. That is until the waiter brought a small ramekin of olives to the table.

I speared one with a cocktail stick, and then another. The menu was resting in my left hand while my right went in for a third.

Across the table Vince sniggered, making me look up.

'Are you hungry, Felicity?' he asked, flicking his eyes to the olives.

I moved my menu to look down. There was only one left. Somehow, I'd eaten them all, my side plate now covered in a small mound of pips. His plate had none.

As my cheeks coloured, I replied grumpily, 'I expected to be eating some time ago, Mr Slater.'

'Mr Slater,' he echoed with a raised eyebrow. 'You know this is a date, right? How about if you call me Vince?' Yet again his pirate's smile was in place, a mix of amusement, outright cheek, a wolfish need to tease and somehow also a threat of desire.

I narrowed my eyes at him. 'Stop looking at me like that.'

'Like what?' he asked, his expression now beginning to smoulder. I could feel my cheeks radiating heat.

'Like you want to cover me in toffee sauce and eat me with a spoon,' I snapped irritably and as quietly as I could. 'I am not dessert, Mr Slater. Nor any other course on your menu. I agreed to this date because I was coerced into it.'

I got a smile and a nod in reply. 'I honestly didn't expect you to show up. I called you earlier because you were fifteen minutes late and I wanted to confirm I could get on and order myself something to eat. That you are here fills me with hope.'

'Hope?' I repeated, not liking the way he said the word.

Again, the smile. It made my stomach writhe. Not with nausea, but fear. Perhaps fear is too harsh of a word, but it was something akin to that.

'Yes, Felicity, hope.' He dropped his voice so it was a soft caress of a whisper. 'I hope to get to know you.' Gone was the rogue, banished so the real Vince could make an appearance. Across from me now, the man looking at me had chosen to drop his guard. His hopeful look, the depth of compassion in his eyes shocked me in a way I just wasn't prepared for.

He reached out with his hand, laying it palm up on the table so I could put my hand into his. Instinctively, as another human bared their soul, I did so, feeling the warmth of his skin on mine. My hand was tiny in his as his fingers closed and he held my gaze, neither of us saying anything.

'You want to get to know me?' I repeated. This tender approach was not what I expected at all.

'Of course, Felicity,' he replied, his eyes locked on mine. Uninvited, unexpected, and largely unwanted, my heart was beginning to race again. 'You are brilliant, talented, graceful, and beautiful.' I would never admit to being any of those things, but it was nice to hear him say it. Abruptly, the pirate's smile returned, 'Besides, how else will I lure you into my bed?'

I snatched my hand back with an exasperated gasp and snatched up my handbag. I was storming out of this restaurant and never speaking to Vince Slater again. Honestly, his brazenness was shocking.

'Come on, Felicity,' he chuckled, seemingly unconcerned that other diners were staring our way and murmuring to one another. 'You enjoyed that kiss and you know it.'

'You stole that kiss!' I snapped. 'I never even saw it coming.'

'Why did you kiss me back then?' he smiled at me ever so knowingly.

My mouth opened to retort, but I didn't have an answer for him. I wanted to say that I hadn't, but conjuring the memory into my mind, I knew that I had. His lips met mine in the dark and I pushed back with my own.

Pausing, while across the room I could see the Maître D urging the doorman to fetch my coat, I met Vince's eyes, and claimed quite triumphantly. 'Savour it. It's the only kiss you will ever get.'

Then I spun on my heel and marched to the door. Around me in the restaurant there were bemused looking men sat at tables with their wives or girlfriends. The women, however, did not look bemused. They were giving me nods of appreciation and support. I think I even saw one woman raise her fist as if punching the air.

My exit from the restaurant would have gone ever so much better if Chief Inspector Quinn hadn't come through the door just before I got to it.

'Ah, Mrs Philips, good evening,' he said, blocking my exit with his body. Two more officers, both men, came in behind him.

Cautiously, since he appeared to be here looking for me, I replied with, 'Good evening.'

'Felicity Philips, I am arresting you for the crime of murder. You do not have to say anything, but it may harm your defence if you do not mention, when questioned, something which you later rely on in court.'

Arrested

My eyes went wide in shock as the world began to spin beneath my feet. I must have heard the words spoken a thousand times watching cop shows with Archie but only heard them spoken by a real police officer for the first time last weekend. I heard them again this morning when the chief inspector took John Ramsey into custody.

Now they were aimed at me. My head went whirly, and I felt my knees sag. Someone caught me, hoisting me into the air with a strong arm under my legs and another around my back. Through the sparkly lights dancing in front of my eyes, I looked up to find Vince's face looking down at me.

That pirate's smile was back where it ought not to be and just before I fainted, he said, 'Adventure, Felicity. That's what you and I have ahead of us.'

When I came to, I was in a side room of the restaurant. Not that I knew where I was instantly; I had to figure it out from the clues.

Feeling groggy, I levered myself into a sitting position. I was in a small room, stretched out on a couch – a staff breakroom I guessed.

'She's awake, sir,' a voice said. I looked up to find one of the male police officers sitting on a plastic chair from where he had been keeping an eye on me.

Other noises drifted in through the door, a murmur of conversation from the restaurant, the squawk and bleep of police radios and the voice of Chief Inspector Quinn as he issued an order to someone before reappearing in the doorway.

'Get her up then, Constable Hayes. Let's go.' He didn't bother to spare me a look.

The young officer rose from his chair, coming toward me as he reached behind his back to produce a set of cuffs.

I waved a horrified arm at him. 'What? What is going on? You said murder!' I squeaked at the chief inspector where he hovered still just outside the door.

He swung his gaze to meet my eyes. 'Yes, Mrs Philips. You were very sloppy. The carpark is littered with CCTV cameras, so too the street outside. It took minutes to find footage showing you tampering with John Ramsey's car and no longer to track your casual stroll to this restaurant to get dinner. I have met plenty of stone-cold killers in my time, but none that managed to portray such innocence as you.'

'But I am innocent!' I protested instantly. 'Hold on,' what he had said finally dawned on me. 'Has something happened to John Ramsey?'

The chief inspector narrowed his eyes at me, then looked up at his constable with an impatient glare. 'To the station, Hayes. I will interview her myself.'

He turned and walked away, leaving me behind with the young constable who put cold steel handcuffs on my delicate wrists. I kept hoping I might wake up from what had to be a nightmare. Perhaps Amber was lying across my face and my brain was being starved of oxygen.

'Where's Vince Slater?' I asked, my voice barely a whisper as the police officer led me through the restaurant.

Somehow, waiting at the door, the chief inspector heard my question. 'Your accomplice is already on his way to the station, Mrs Philips.' He added nothing further, the accusations ringing in my head enough to clamour out all noise but the rushing of blood to my head and the thumping beat in my chest.

67

I was mortified to have been arrested, terrified that I might be found guilty because I *had* been near John Ramsey's car, and just about bright enough to keep my mouth shut.

On the way to the station, all manner of questions and thoughts whirled around like a maelstrom in my mind. Secured in the back of a police car and trying hard to stop myself hyperventilating, I focused on what I might need to say, on what I had actually done, and who I could call.

I didn't have a lawyer at my beck and call. Who does? There were legal firms in my contacts list but that was for ensuring contracts were legally binding when I took on my clients. Securing some of the biggest wedding venues, ordering dresses that cost the same as a car ... all these things are managed by me or rather, by my firm, and when spending that kind of cash in an environment where one in ten engagements never make it to the ceremony, both parties need protection.

Anyway, they were not the right people, but I suspected they would know someone who was. I hadn't killed John Ramsey. I hadn't even wanted him dead. Not since we were kids anyway. Any decent criminal defence lawyer would be able to clear this up in a few hours. That's what I told myself in the dark shadows of that police car and whether it was a lie for my own benefit or not, it made me feel a little better.

At the station, I was processed, my fingerprints taken, and my personal belongings removed. It was when they got to my handbag that a fresh spike of panic shot through me. In my handbag were the pages of numbers I'd lifted from John's car. It served as evidence of wrong doing, though if the chief inspector's claim to have CCTV footage of me was true I doubted the pages would be any more damning, but perhaps they would show that all I did was steal something.

It was hardly a demonstration of innocence, but it was a long way from murder too.

The pages weren't in my handbag though. The sergeant behind the desk, a flat-chested woman with a stern face and short hair cropped in a man's style went through the contents of my handbag one item at a time. The pages were not there.

Perplexed, and wondering what to make of it, I kept quiet, believing the fewer words I said the better off I might be.

Vince was nowhere in sight, but when a constable – another woman – this one in her twenties but bearing the same professional disinterest in me, took me to the row of cells, I could hear his voice echoing out. He was singing. It was *Jail Guitar Doors* by *The Clash*, a song I hadn't heard in more than thirty years. That I could name it startled me, but back in my teenage years, I had been into that dirty rock music.

In the back of my head as I walked into my cell, a voice laughed that Vince and I had the same taste in music.

I said some rude things to that voice.

I genuinely didn't expect to fall asleep. The rigid, hard shelf that formed a bed was the only thing to sit on. It was far from comfortable, but I guess my eyes got heavy because the sound of the cell door opening woke me.

Looking in was an emotionless police constable in his forties. He had a thick beard with a few specs of white invading the dark brown and glasses that seemed to have been colour matched to his hair. Using two fingers, he motioned for me to leave the cell and then walk ahead of him. I got mostly single word commands telling me to, 'Wait,' or, 'Turn right,' until I found myself out of the cell area.

The constable said, 'Stop.' He had led me to a door marked Interview Room 2. Butterflies erupted in my stomach. I hadn't been here long, just over an hour according to the clock on the wall, but wasn't I supposed to be given a phone call and see a lawyer before I had to speak with anyone?

The bearded, bespectacled constable knocked on the interview room door, got an invitation to enter, and pushed it open.

Chief Inspector Quinn was inside. 'Please, come in, Mrs Philips,' he beckoned. 'Can I offer you a cup of tea? I understand from Mr Slater that we arrived before you got a chance to eat your dinner Can I have someone bring you a sandwich?'

It felt like a trap, but my stomach rumbled audibly again which made it seem churlish to refuse. 'Thank you, Chief Inspector. Tea and a sandwich would be most welcome.'

The constable at the door got a nod and closed the door, departing to fetch my snack and drink, I hoped.

Since Quinn was acting friendly, I chose to broach the subject of my arrest.

'You don't really think I had anything to do with whatever happened to John Ramsey, surely?'

He shuffled some paperwork on the desk to his front, refusing to make eye contact. 'Take a seat, please, Mrs Philips.'

I did, staring at his head until he looked up and met my eyes.

'Well? Do you?' I wanted to know. 'Because the idea is ludicrous.'

Sitting by his side was a sergeant. Tall, clean-shaven like Quinn but with ginger hair, he spoke next, talking to a computerised recording device to announce the interview and those present.

When his sergeant stopped talking, Quinn asked, 'Is it ludicrous, Mrs Philips? You admitted to having a long history of ill-feeling toward John Ramsey. You went out of your way to ensure he was trapped at the Bleakwith residence earlier today and this evening you tracked him to his place of work and can be seen tampering with his car.'

'I wasn't tampering with it!' I felt shocked at the repeated claim. 'I was … I wanted to confirm it was his car. I was meeting Vince for dinner at The Wild Oak. You can check our reservation.'

'I already did,' the chief inspector replied. 'You do realise that suggests this was premeditated?'

'What!' Each time he spoke, it was like another slap to the face. 'I saw John's car and was surprised. I thought you would have him in custody still and I wanted to check it was his car,' I was getting flustered and repeating myself. 'And then I saw something on his passenger seat and …'

'Yes,' Chief Inspector Quinn encouraged.

'Well.' I knew I was opening a trap door with what I was going to say next. 'It looked like it might be a clue.'

The sergeant sniggered. A small laugh escaping his lips. The chief inspector didn't laugh.

'A clue,' he repeated. 'To what exactly, Mrs Philips?'

Okay he had me there. 'To whatever is going on,' I hazarded, not even managing to convince myself. 'Look, I don't know what is happening, but when Vince and I were inside Orion Printing, we overheard someone talking about erasing evidence. If John Ramsey pushed Derek Bleakwith over his balcony, why did he do it? Something is going on and I think you should be trying to find out what it is, not hassling me. If you hadn't let him go, I wouldn't have seen John Ramsey's car and we wouldn't be sitting here now.'

The chief inspector let me finish, steadfastly allowing me to run my idiot mouth which should have been clamped shut, I suddenly realised. Why hadn't I demanded to have a lawyer present? Why had I spoken at all? I bet myself Patricia Fisher wouldn't have said a word.

Leaning forward in his chair to get his face closer to mine, Chief Inspector Quinn said, 'So you admit to breaking and entering the premises of Orion Printing?'

My cheeks flushed bright red. 'I want to speak to my lawyer.'

'Do you have a lawyer?' Quinn asked.

'Um. I can get one,' I tried to sound confident but didn't think I achieved the level I was aiming for.

'Your rights were read to you at the time of your arrest, Mrs Philips,' he stated calmly. 'Would you like to make a phone call?'

I am such an amateur. Blabbing on and on, telling the chief inspector everything he wanted to know instead of using my head. Now I was probably in deeper than I had been when they first arrested me.

Who on Earth did I call though? Escorted from the interview, which was terminated pending my return with legal representation later, I found myself jittery with nerves. I needed someone to swoop in to save me from this mess.

It was the monosyllabic bearded constable who came back to get me. He had my sandwich and cup of tea and managed to speak a few words finally to tell me I couldn't have them in my cell so would have to stand in the corridor to consume them or not have them at all.

Treated like a common criminal, and feeling like one too, I took a slurp of the going-cold tea and tore the sandwich from its plastic wrapper. Being watched, I refused to feel self-conscious, and despite the rather stale bread and dubious unidentifiable meat filling, I ate the whole thing and felt glad to have something to fill the hole in my middle.

Beardy took my empty cup and plastic wrapper, then led me to a phone mounted on a wall. It was an old thing like one used to find in a public call box.

'There are numbers for lawyers on the wall,' Beardy pointed out. I twitched my eyes at a board covered in business cards, but I already knew who I was about to call. For some reason, it hadn't occurred to me until I was chewing my sandwich, but unbidden the memory surfaced – my brother-in-law is a lawyer.

My Sister and I do not see eye to eye on anything and never have. She is a bully who has always tried to rub my face in her superior height and superior looks. She was happy to point out her husband's superior job. Anywhere she could score a point, she did. Since we were little girls living in the same house, she always had a reason to pick on me.

Of course, I believe the reason is because she is a horrible cow, but I wasn't going to point that out right now because I needed her for once.

Mercifully, hers was one of the numbers I had etched in my memory. It was after eleven; late, but not so late that I thought she might be asleep.

'Ginny Walters,' she answered the phone, wondering who might be calling this late and on a number she didn't recognise.

'Ginny,' I bit my lip and cursed my luck. She would call mum the moment she got off the phone to me and would ride my incarceration like a bad anecdote for the next decade. 'It's Felicity. I need your help.'

It was a simple statement and one designed to interrupt whatever she was about to say next - I rarely got to finish a sentence before my big sister would start to talk about herself. For once I managed to silence her, even if not for long.

'You need my help,' she repeated. Her tone turned suspicious. 'Why? What with?'

I sucked in a deep breath and got the words out before I changed my mind. 'I've been arrested for murder. I need Shane.'

Several seconds of silence followed. Enough that I drew a breath to ask if she was still there.

She spoke before I could. 'I see. Well, I have to say this doesn't shock me.'

'What? My getting arrested and accused of murder doesn't shock you? I'm a wedding planner, Ginny. Why would you ever think I might get arrested for murder?' With our history, it didn't take much for my rage level to spike.

Ginny snapped, 'Do you want me to help you or not?' She was enjoying her position of power, just the way I knew she would.

'Yes,' I replied with a reluctant sigh.

'Yes, what?' She was going to make me beg. The horrible old witch was genuinely going to make me beg when my very freedom was on the line.

'Please, Ginny,' I begged, imploring her to stop messing me around. 'I'm in Maidstone police station. I need Shane's help and I need it now.' I was almost at the point of tears, the evening proving too much for my gentle spirit to take. I wasn't hardened against such experiences the way Vince seemed to be.

Sounding bored, Ginny said, 'I'll see what I can do,' and with that she put the phone down. I was left standing in the corridor with Beardy watching me while I stared incomprehensibly at the phone. The dial tone mocked me, but my one call was complete, and I was going nowhere except back to my cell.

I awoke shivering in the dark some hours later, but it was the sound of the viewing hatch being opened and closed that woke me and my door was being unlocked now that whoever was outside had confirmed I wasn't poised to attack behind the door.

It was Beardy again, whose name I still didn't know and guiltily had not attempted to learn. 'Come on,' he beckoned. 'You're being released.'

The news propelled me from the bed and onto the cold floor of the cell.

'Released? As in I can go home?'

'That's usually what released means,' he replied flippantly while waiting for me to straighten my clothes.

I didn't waste any time getting out of the cell, slipping my shoes back on and hurrying through the door while still rearranging myself. Immediately buoyed by the prospect of having the charges against me dropped, I was disappointed to find myself back outside Interview Room 2.

'I thought I was being released?' I questioned.

I got a nod from Beardy. 'Once you have spoken with the chief inspector.'

He did the knock, wait, push the door open thing, but to my great relief, when the door swung to reveal the room, my brother-in-law was sitting opposite Chief Inspector Quinn. I could not remember ever being more glad to see anyone in my life.

He was getting to his feet and I all but knocked him back into his chair when I flung my arms around him.

'Good morning, Felicity,' he said with a chuckle. 'Don't worry, we will be leaving shortly. The chief inspector just has a few things to say first.' He dropped the amused tone he used on me. 'Don't you chief inspector?' Shane growled.

What was going on? I didn't know my brother-in-law very well because he was married to my sister and thus I hardly ever spent any time in his company. Ginny and I avoided each other. Or possibly it was the case that I avoided her while never making it into her conscious thought as a thing that even existed.

Either way, I knew he was a lawyer and a barrister and went to court but beyond that I couldn't have said anything about his career. However, he was acting like he owned the room and the chief inspector … well, he looked cowed almost. Annoyed too, his eyes and top lip twitching as if something were deeply aggravating him.

'Can we hurry this along, Chief Inspector?' Shane demanded. 'I am due in court in an hour.'

Snapping his head and eyes across to glare at me, Chief Inspector Quinn's lips were pressed together so hard that they looked like they might just merge into one.

It would be an improvement if he couldn't talk. The naughty voice in my head was back because I no longer felt utterly terrified.

'I owe you an apology, Mrs Philips,' the chief inspector announced, and I thought I might just fall off my chair I was that surprised. 'There were some … discrepancies in my investigation.' The chair to his left, which last night had a sergeant in it, was now empty, the chief inspector wanting no one to hear him admit his error. 'You are, of course, free to go.' He fell silent.

No one said anything for a second, but just when I was going to speak, planning to graciously accept his apology, Shane placed a hand on my arm.

'And?' he prompted.

The chief inspector's top lip twitched in annoyance again. 'And I am sorry for any inconvenience this has caused. Shortly, I will be issuing a statement to the effect that you were mistakenly arrested.'

I waited to see if there was any more to come and glanced at Shane for a nod that we were done before saying. 'Thank you, Chief Inspector. I hope you catch whoever did kill john Ramsey.'

The lip twitched again, but he said nothing, getting to his feet to open the door. Exposed to the people beyond – his people – he put on a smile and offered me his hand to shake.

The naughty voice told me to slap it away, but I extended my own, thinking it probably better to let the man save some face rather than make an enemy of him.

Clearly primed, Beardy was waiting to escort me back to where my possessions were catalogued and taken away the previous evening. Five minutes later, I had everything back and packed inside my handbag. My coat was back on my shoulders and I was leaving the police station with a plan to never ever return.

I barely spoke at any point, however, once we were outside the torrent of questions building mass in my head burst forth like a dam breaking.

'Oh, my goodness! How did you get him to apologise? What discrepancy was there? What happened to John Ramsey; no one told me? I got arrested with Vince Slater, do you know if they let him out?'

Shane laughed and held up both hands to slow me down. 'Whoa, Nelly. The crux of this is that the chief inspector didn't wait for the forensic team to examine the car. I believe he reacted the moment he heard about the crash. It was on the news because it closed off the motorway heading south.'

I wasn't following what Shane was trying to tell me.

Seeing my confusion, Shane explained. 'The brakes failed on John Ramsey's car. The verdict recorded is accidental death.'

The news took me by surprise. 'So he wasn't murdered at all?'

Shane frowned slightly. 'No, Felicity. The point being that the chief inspector was more than a little premature in his desire to arrest you. How can you be charged with murder when no one had been murdered?'

'Hence the apology.'

Shane nodded. 'What you don't know is that the chief inspector has a couple of black marks against him already. He's a clever operator and a good policeman; nothing ever sticks, but if enough mud gets thrown … He has his eyes set on one of the top jobs. Maybe even the top job of Commissioner and I reminded him of the need to appear to be squeaky clean.'

'You mean you threatened him?' I gasped.

Shane snorted a small laugh. 'Not exactly. I have cross examined him in the past while defending my clients and thus far I have always come out on top.'

'What about breaking into Orion Print? I admitted to doing it.' I really was dumb.

'Actually, you were lucky to get away without being cautioned for that, Felicity. It would seem that your ... friend, Mr Slater,' Shane wasn't sure how to label Vince, 'claimed he heard a cry for help and upon investigation discovered the rear door to the property to be open. With the embarrassment of the false murder charge against him, it was in the chief inspector's best interest to let the possible B&E charge go. It's not as if he had any evidence. I don't for one minute think the chief inspector believed him, but Mr Slater's counsel had no trouble getting him released.'

'Vince is out too?' I looked around, wondering whether he was still here waiting for me.

Shane nodded. 'Listen, I got you out, but I doubt that will be the end of it.'

Fear shot through me. 'What do you mean?'

'Well, for a start, Chief Inspector Quinn is a sore loser. He will be watching you because he still thinks you are guilty. The accidental death verdict can be reversed easily if they find sufficient reason to doubt it. I forced him to back off, but that will just mean he now applies extra effort to find the evidence. He'll have a team working on the CCTV footage, trying to manipulate it so they can see what you did to John Ramsey's car.'

'I didn't do anything to it,' I protested, failing to mention that I stole paperwork from it.

He puffed out his cheeks. 'That won't matter either. Quinn is going to look for a way to catch you out. My advice is to go back to work, immerse

80

yourself in your job and act as if nothing happened. Now, sorry, but I must dash. I really do have to be in court in an hour, Felicity. Is there anything you need?'

I needed a shower and a change of clothes. Something for breakfast would be nice and maybe a chiropractor to straighten my spine after sleeping on what the police believe can pass for a bed. I shook my head. 'No, Shane. Thank you for coming to my rescue. You'll have to send me a bill for your services.'

'Nonsense,' he laughed at me. 'You are family.' He shot his cuff to check his watch, grimacing when he did.

'Go,' I insisted. 'I'm heading for home. Don't worry about me, I'll be fine now that I am out of that awful place.'

He smiled at me, but wasted no further words, hurrying away to get on with his day.

Standing outside Maidstone police station wearing yesterday's clothes and with hair that must look a terrible state, I was attracting the attention of passing motorists. Goodness only knows what they might imagine had befallen me. I had to look a sight and needed to get out of the public eye before someone spotted me.

Of course, my car was still in Aylesford, parked behind Orion Print. I could walk there, but I was going to find a taxi instead. Aylesford is a quiet village so I wasn't worried that anything might have happened to it during the night.

I got about three feet when a car about to drive by me in the road abruptly braked. The suddenness of it, with an accompanying squeal of tyres made me jump. It was on the two-lane ring road running around the city and nearly caused a pile up as the cars following had to slam on their own brakes to avoid a collision. Horns blared and the air turned blue with shouted insults as motorists told the driver causing all the fuss what they thought.

I had no idea why the car had stopped and was just starting on my way again when a voice stopped me.

'Oh, my goodness! It was true!'

The voice made me cringe. There was a part of me that knew I ought to put my head down and run, but too dumb to obey my instincts, I let my anger rule instead.

'Primrose,' I growled, turning to face the woman now getting out of her car. Primrose Green owns and runs Kent's second most successful wedding boutique and wants nothing more in life than to hold the number one spot. She's six inches taller, twenty years younger, two cup sizes bigger, and has the face and figure of a former model because that is exactly what she is. She's also married with two perfect children and none of it would be a problem if she wasn't such a terrible person.

Drivers continued to blast their horns and offer opinion at the hold up she had caused, but Primrose was completely oblivious. She was coming toward me with her phone in her hand, but it was only when she started taking pictures that I realised what she was trying to do.

Primrose has no good way to beat me in the wedding game, so she resorts to dirty tactics instead. An image of me looking dishevelled outside a police station would somehow make it into one of her ad campaigns with an equally undeserved and unpleasant headline.

I threw my arms in front of my face to stop her getting what she wanted.

'I knew it!' she cackled happily. 'I knew you were doing something criminal. There is no way you keep getting the top clients fairly. What is it, Felicity? Have you been finding out the celebrities' dirty secrets and blackmailing them? Or are you doing deals under the table?' She gasped. 'Is it drugs? Please tell me it's drugs. Hey!'

Her tone changed at the last word, her fascination and amusement vanishing to be replaced by indignant outrage.

'Give that back!' she demanded.

I had been hiding my face and attempting to get away as she pursued me down the street, but I risked a glance now to see what might be happening.

The impeccably dressed Primrose was being held at bay by one long left arm, the owner's palm facing out to ward her off. At full stretch in the other direction was her phone, the top of it visible above the fingers of the right hand.

Both hands belonged to Vince Slater. I took a moment to look up at the sky and ask why I was being punished.

'Give me back my phone!' Primrose shouted. 'I'll scream for help,' she threatened. We're right in front of a police station.'

Vince laughed at her. 'Yes, we are. I note you are illegally parked on a main thoroughfare and appear to be stalking Mrs Philips.' He turned his head in my direction. 'Here, catch.'

The phone was in the air the next second, my eyes flaring in surprise as it arced toward me. I had to dart forward to snatch it from the air, almost dropping it twice before juggling it safely into my palms.

'You may wish to erase the pictures she took,' suggested Vince.

Primrose was incensed. 'That's mine. The pictures on it belong to me.' She was trying to go around Vince, but he was twice as wide, a hundred pounds heavier (at least), and found her attempts to get to me amusing.

She hit him with her handbag, and he burst out laughing.

The front door of the police station opened, two cops sticking their heads out. I recognised them as the ones manning the front desk.

'Whose car is that?' one demanded to know.

'It's hers,' I supplied happily while pressing delete on the last of the pictures she'd taken. She'd managed to snap several terrible ones before I realised what she was doing and thought to hide my face.

'Are you broken down?' the cop enquired, his tone making it clear he didn't for one second believe she was.

Primrose's face coloured as she tried to bluff.

Vince asked, 'Done?'

I handed him the phone.

He turned, grabbed Primrose's left wrist, and slapped the phone back into her hand. Giving her as much attention as one might a piece of litter blowing on the breeze, he left her there, putting an arm out to guide me away.

His voice low, he told me, 'I have a car in the car park along the street. Let's be somewhere else, eh?'

I was going to get in his car, quite willingly, in fact. I could not, however, deny the feeling that I was the fly accepting the spider's invitation.'

Mating

Acting in a manner which to me seemed uncharacteristically helpful and charming, Vince drove the threeish miles to Aylesford to drop me next to my car. It was, as expected, just as I left it.

I thanked him for his generosity and started to get out. It was then that a question occurred to me.

'I took some pages from John's car last night. They were financial statements. When I got to the police station they were no longer in my handbag. Did you take them?'

Vince did a good job of looking shocked by my question. 'Goodness, Felicity. Of course not.'

I hurriedly apologised. 'Sorry. I … it was wrong of me to ask. Thank you for returning me to my car,' I thanked him again. 'I'll, um. I'll just go. Sorry.' Ashamed for thinking the worst of him when I had no good reason to, I got out of his car and dug around in my handbag for my keys.

Vince got out as well, hanging half in and half out to look over his door until I was getting into mine.

'Do you want to hear about what happened to John Ramsey?' he asked.

'He crashed his car. I know that already.'

Vince shook his head, a knowing smile stuck to his face. 'Yes and no. That's not the full story.'

Narrowing my eyes, I bit the hook. 'Go on then. What's the full story?'

He didn't give me an answer, he asked another question. 'Are you going home now?'

Frowning, I said, 'Yes. I need to see to my pets and sort myself out. I feel scuzzy.'

He started to duck back into his car. 'Super. I'll follow you. I'll tell you all about it over breakfast.'

Before I could argue, he ducked back into his car to leave me staring at him through his windscreen. He winked at me.

When I didn't move, he stuck his head out of his car again. 'Come along, Felicity. It will take too long to explain it all now and I'm sure you want to get home.'

Not waiting for me to respond, he backed his car up and turned it around so it faced out toward the road again. Getting in my car while grinding my back teeth against each other, I resolved to find a way to make Mr Slater lose his interest in me. Yes, he kept saving me from various foes, but if I spent much more time in his company, I was going to get an ulcer.

Muttering under my breath, I slumped into my car, fired up the engine and led the way. My Mercedes SL500 is a nifty little thing, lightweight and flat to the road, it turns fast and takes off like a smacked cat when required. I put that to use, taking Vince on a countryside route where I promptly lost him behind the first tractor I could find.

Far slower in his big SUV, he didn't have the acceleration to slingshot around it. You might think me ungrateful, but I laughed as I watched him disappear in my rear-view mirror.

Arriving home at what would be my usual time to get up, I was tired but wanted only to fall into my normal Friday routine – a swift shower, walk Buster, grab a quick breakfast, and head for work. The tenacious Mr

Slater would undoubtedly turn up at my boutique later, but by then, and on my own turf, I might feel better equipped to deal with him.

I heard Buster woofing the moment my tyres crunched over the gravel and a twitch of the curtain showed me where Amber had just been.

What Buster had to say was not fit for repeating but did require a response when I got through the door.

'I was not out mating all night,' I insisted sternly.

Buster was barking and bouncing on the spot, but my statement stopped him.

Eyeing me quizzically, he asked, '*Where were you then?*'

Putting my bag down on the narrow console table just inside the door, and starting to shuck my coat, I replied, 'I was locked in a jail cell, if you must know.' Hanging the coat up, I took a pace to push the door shut.

'*Wait,*' said Buster, darting for the gap. '*I need to go.*'

He probably did, the poor thing. He missed his usual last-thing-before-bed excursion and had to have been holding it all night.

He shot through the door. Then just as I was going to close it to keep the cool air outside, he shoved his head back around the edge to look up at me.

'*When you go in the living room, just remember that you love me, okay?*'

My eyes widened. 'What did you do?'

He started to back out through the door again, adding, '*Remember our love when you go in the kitchen too.*'

Fearful for what destruction he might have wrought, I closed the door and went to see.

Amber sashayed out of the living room just as I got to it.

'You will insist on letting him live in the house,' she chided, basically reminding me that whatever I found was my fault.

Going into my living room, I couldn't decide if my eyes should be wide to take it all in or peering through my fingers so I could absorb it just a piece at a time.

There was a lot of fluff. It could have been much worse. A casual inspection suggested one of my throw pillows had bought the farm in a spectacular way. I might be able to understand what he had to say, but I was never going to work out why he did the things he did. I guess when all is said and done, he is just a dog. A youngish one at that.

Tidying up the mess could wait. I went to see if the kitchen had fared worse.

Amber was on the kitchen counter, next to the cupboard that contained her food. *'He refuses to use the litter tray, Felicity. Perhaps a kennel if you cannot get on board with the euthanasia idea?'*

Over by the back door, was something I couldn't leave for later. Not that I wanted to deal with it now either. Curling my lip, I went in search of rubber gloves, spray disinfectant, and toilet tissue.

It really wasn't his fault; I was the one who didn't come home. As for the litter tray, I couldn't imagine what might happen to it if he were to attempt to use it. I thought it most likely he would put one paw on the edge and flip the contents across the room.

I didn't dwell too long on that mental image.

With the flick of a finger, the coffee machine was pressed into service and I walked back through the house unbuttoning my blouse as I went. I was more than ready for a shower. My bedroom is first on the left next to the front door, convenient for letting Buster out into the garden late at night and first thing in the morning. He always sleeps next to my bed anyway.

Dropping my blouse into the hamper, I started to fiddle with my bra. I managed to dislocate my left shoulder a week ago and mundane tasks like taking off my bra were proving difficult still. Buster was wandering back past my window heading for the door so I wandered out of the bedroom to crack the front door open again.

'Let yourself in,' I called.

'Sure thing,' said Vince.

I screamed in terror at the unexpected voice and spun on the spot just as the catch on my bra came free.

Vince's eyes went wide just as a grin spread across his face.

Buster popped his head between Vince's legs. '*I found Vince outside,*' he said helpfully.

Mortified yet again, I darted into my bedroom, holding my chest with both hands while shouting several unladylike things.

'Shall I shut the door?' Vince enquired conversationally.

'Yes, please,' I growled back. 'Make sure you are on the outside first though.'

Far from achieving the desired effect, I heard the door shut but his chuckling was clearly coming from inside my cottage.

'I think I can hear a coffee machine getting excited. 'I'll make us a cup each, shall I?' he asked, then added. 'Unless, you know, since you are already half naked and flashing the goods around ...'

'One more word, Vince Slater,' I warned. 'One more word and I will call the police.'

'Be sure to ask for Chief Inspector Quinn,' he sniggered at me. Seconds later, he was whistling a happy tune in my kitchen and I could hear him going through my cupboards in search of food. He was cooing to Amber and ... well, let's just say I was having fantasies about his head and my meat tenderiser.

I took a shower, locking the door and shifting the laundry hamper under the door handle so it wouldn't open. By the time I came out, the house was filled with the glorious scent of coffee.

And bacon?

Why could I smell bacon?

Wanting to get dressed but too curious now to wait, I wrapped myself in a robe, stuffed my feet in slippers and went to find the unlovable rogue.

'Your dog likes bacon, doesn't he?' Vince observed as I came into the room. He was leaning against the breakfast bar end of the kitchen's central island. Next to his arm was a plate that was mostly crumbs but had the remaining corner of a toasted bacon sandwich to one side. Loose pieces of bacon were stacked on a separate side plate and one hung from his fingers while Buster danced on his back legs trying to get to it.

Vince dropped it. It fell into the black hole Buster called a mouth and was gone.

'I made enough for you,' Vince smiled at me. 'Your coffee is good too,' he let me know as he picked up his mug for a slurp.

Amber was on a different counter, not watching the display the dog was putting on as he begged for another piece of glistening meat. She was licking a paw and studying it but looked up to make eye contact with me.

'*This is the one you were mating with?*' she asked. '*He gave me sardines. I actually … yes, I actually approve. He can move in.*'

'He is not moving in!' I huffed.

Vince looked up. 'I'm sorry, what? You want me to move in?'

I narrowed my eyes at the cat. Not that it had any effect.

Buster swallowed another piece of bacon and said, '*Yeah. The cat and I agree for once. Do all the mating you like with this one. He's great.*'

I could feel a migraine coming.

The time to deal with my pets was later. First, I had to get the man with the pirate smile out of my house. 'How did you find me?'

He popped the last of his bacon sandwich in his mouth before answering, chewing it still when he found some words. 'I fitted a tracker to your car.'

I nearly choked.

That just made him laugh again. 'Only kidding,' he assured me.

I was going to have someone check my car later, believe me.

'I looked up your home address. I mean, that's using my initiative, that is. Tired and stuff, I figured you forgot I was following but I promised to tell you about John Ramsey and that's what I came here to do.'

'Really?' I didn't bother to hide my suspicion. 'You'll tell me what happened and then you'll leave?'

I got a questioning look in response. 'Of course. What kind of man do you think I am?'

'A pirate in a good suit,' I replied without needing to think.

It was his turn to choke, the bacon sandwich going down the wrong hole as he spluttered with laughter. He had to turn around to sort himself out, and when he turned back there were tears streaking down his cheeks. 'A pirate in a good suit,' he repeated my words. 'Oh, my. That is a good one.'

Becoming increasingly irritated by my 'guest', I said, 'Please tell me about John Ramsey, Mr Slater.'

'His brakes didn't fail. Someone messed with them,' Vince replied taking another slurp of his coffee.

Suddenly wanting my own, I found one already poured and waiting when I looked.

'Black, two sweeteners, right?' Vince confirmed.

'How do you know that?' I narrowed my eyes at him.

'I have people spying on you,' he told me deadpan. This time I didn't bite, and he rolled his eyes playfully. 'You were drinking coffee at Loxton Hall last weekend. I get paid to be observant.'

'Okay.' I wasn't entirely satisfied by his explanation. 'I heard his brakes failed. They recorded his death as accidental. It's why we were released, was it not? What makes you think this was murder after all?'

He put his coffee cup down and dabbed at his lips with a handkerchief before saying. 'I have a couple of friends in the police. We scratch each other's backs. John Ramsey's brakes failed because someone had loosened the bleed nipple on the front left calliper. Apparently, it was open just enough for the brake fluid to drip out under pressure. Each time he used the brakes, his lost a little more fluid. When the reservoir emptied, no more brakes.'

I didn't know what to make of this news. 'How come the chief inspector let us go then?'

'I guess because it is only conjecture. I am guessing his brakes were fiddled with. I've never heard of a bleed nipple coming undone by itself. Have you?'

I wasn't sure what a bleed nipple was, and I didn't like the shark-infested smile that teased his lips when he said the word 'nipple' though he managed to keep his eyes from looking down to where mine were hidden beneath the robe. He'd already seen far more of me than I ever intended.

'So you think someone deliberately tampered with his car. Someone who knew exactly how much to open the bleed,' I forced myself to say the word, 'nipple.'

Vince tried but failed to push his grin away. He nodded though. 'Unfortunately, there are a lot of people who have a high enough knowledge of car mechanics to be able to do that.'

I looked at the clock on my cooker and blew out a breath. 'Right, so there is a homicidal mechanic out there and he killed John Ramsey. John tried to kill Derek Bleakwith, and there is someone at the Orion Print office trying to cover up the evidence of something they were doing.' Remembering the data drive I looked up at Vince.

He knew what I was going to say. 'The police confiscated it. The second they saw it had files and data on it from Orion Print, I knew I would struggle to justify having it in my possession. I told them I picked it up out of interest when we were looking for the person we heard calling for help.'

I skewed my lips to one side as I studied him. 'How did you know to say that to the police? How did you know it would muddy the water enough to get you off?'

'Experience, babe,' the pirate's grin returned.

My eyes were already narrowed. In fact, I'd been squinting at him for so long my face was starting to hurt.

'How did you get the back door open? It wasn't really unlocked was it?'

He bumped away from the counter with his hip. 'That's the sort of incriminating answer a man only reveals in bed.'

My jaw dropped open. He was so brazen!

'It is time for you to leave, Mr Slater,' I took a step back to give him easy access to my front door and pointed with my arm. 'You came to tell me about John Ramsey, and you have done so. Now I need to get dressed and get to work.'

He cocked an eyebrow at me. 'Surely we need to track the killer and clear your name? That woman ... what's her name?'

'Primrose?' I hazarded, not sure who he might be referring to.

'Yes, her. You said she would cause you problems and try to scare off clients. We need to get ahead of that and solve this case. The chief inspector thinks you are behind what happened to John.'

That was exactly what Shane said.

Whatever the case, and whatever I chose to do, I was not going to be doing it with Vince Slater.

'Thank you, Mr Slater. But I am a wedding planner, not a private eye. Feel free to do whatever snooping you fancy. I have a big wedding on Raven Island next weekend and a dozen other events in various stages of preparedness. I am much too busy to be poking my nose in anywhere else. I expect the police will figure this out for themselves and prove my innocence soon enough without me having to lift a finger.'

'Final word?' He offered me a chance to change my mind.

I pointed to my front door again. 'Please leave, Mr Slater.'

He smiled and nodded. 'No problem, Felicity. Whatever you say. I'm going to call this mission accomplished anyway.'

Confused, I asked, 'Mission what? What are you saying now?'

He was backing away from me, heading for the door, and spread his arms as a show of innocence. 'Well, the chaps offered me a little wager and I can honestly claim to have won.' He waited for my confusion to deepen. 'I bet them I would get to see you naked and have breakfast at your house.'

The coffee mug smashed into the door half a second after his big, stupid grin vanished behind it.

I allowed myself a second to fume, glaring at the door and half hoping Vince would open it again for one final parting comment because I already had another missile ready in my right hand.

When I heard his car start and the crunch of gravel as he pulled away, I placed the apple I held ready back in my fruit bowl and crossed the kitchen to the coffee machine. I was operating on far less sleep than was usual and felt the caffeine was not only justified but necessary.

I made toast, deciding against the bacon largely because Vince had touched it.

Buster followed me. '*Do you not want the bacon? Because if you are not planning to eat it … actually, even if you are planning to eat it, I think I would benefit enormously from the extra calories and protein.*'

I shot him a look. 'Have you been watching the fitness channel again?'

Amber stopped licking her paw for a moment to say, '*He caught a special on muscle building and now thinks he can turn himself into a Rottweiler if he eats the right food.*'

'*I didn't say Rottweiler,*' snapped Buster. '*But, yes, essentially it is time to up my game. If I want to be a superhero night stalker dog, I need to put on muscle.*'

I looked down at the floor from where Buster looked back up. There were two lines of drool hanging from either side of his mouth. One almost reached to the floor. He gave me a hopeful expression and an idea popped into my head.

I blinked a couple of times and let it go around inside my skull, but it was an idea with merit.

'Amber,' I started, swivelling to face her. She didn't bother to look my way; I was nowhere near as interesting as her paw. 'Would you be willing to do something for me if there was a piece of fresh fish in it for you?'

I was quite willing to admit that as a wedding planner, I had no business attempting to investigate the death of John Ramsey and whatever other crimes were associated with it. Poking my nose where it wasn't wanted hadn't done me much good so far. However, Buster and Amber, and in particular my unique relationship with them, might give me an advantage no one else would have.

Could I solve the crime with the help of my pets? It would put the chief inspector's nose truly out of joint and maybe even wipe that shark-infested grin from Vince's face.

I would be lying if I said the concept wasn't tempting. It was tempting enough that I was already thinking about how I could employ my cat and dog.

When I looked back to see if Amber had even heard me, I found she was staring at me. Giving me her attention was a rarity unless she wanted something and that didn't happen very often.

'*Don't tease me, woman,*' she meowled in warning. '*It's not beyond me to seek revenge if promised gifts do not materialise.*'

She'd never spoken like this before. More usually, it was all I could do to get here to even pay me attention. Had I just discovered the secret trick that would make her do as I ask?

'What sort of fish would you like it to be?' I asked.

The paw she'd been licking still hovered in the air an inch from her face. She placed it back on the counter, fixing me with a serious expression. '*Mackerel. Lightly poached in milk with a bay leaf, the stock or liquor reserved for drinking separately.*'

Oh, yeah, I had her attention now.

'What if I promised to give you the mackerel exactly as you have just described it. Would you be willing to do something for me?'

Amber narrowed her eyes. '*I'm a cat. I already do plenty for you.*'

Scratching his left ear with a back foot, Buster laughed. '*Oh, yeah? Like what?*'

'*I enrich your life just by being here. Unlike the dog, I instil calm and a sense of wellbeing. I brighten any room I choose to enter … must I go on? Does your ignorance not embarrass you?*'

Amber was just being a cat, but she was going to have to dance to my tune if she wanted the poached fish.

'Let me put it another way. What would you do, beyond that which you already do, for the offer of a piece of poached mackerel?'

'*Poached in milk,*' Amber reminded me.

Buster said, '*I'll do anything you ask. I'll do it right now, I'll do it twice, and you only have to give me a gravy bone.*' His stumpy tail wagged incessantly.

I took a gravy bone from the bone-print jar on the counter and threw it to him. It didn't hit the ground.

'A whole mackerel, Amber,' I goaded. I could see she wanted to give in. 'I need you to do a few things for me, that's all.'

Amber was wrestling with her desire for the super-tasty treat and her need to be haughty and dominant.

'*It's the dog's job to do things and run around obeying,*' she replied, but her words had a frustrated edge to them now.

I crossed the room and gave her fur a stroke, smoothing it from head to tail. 'A dog couldn't do the things I need you to do, Amber. These tasks require a level of dexterity and agility only a cat can achieve.' I had her, and she knew it.

'*What do you need me to do?*' she asked, closing her eyes, and leaning into my hand.

Going through what I might need to do in my head, one task leapt to the fore. I needed to find out what Derek knew. He had been away from the office for some time with his ailments, but surely he would have at least an inkling as to what drove John to shove him over the balcony. I would also ask him about what John meant about not being the crook in the equation.

Did John mean it was Derek? Surely not. Then who? And who did I hear destroying evidence last night and what was it evidence of? These questions and more made a long queue in my mind and only Derek would be able to answer them.

I called Joanne, running through what I wanted to say in my head while I waited for the phone to connect.

'Felicity?' Joanne answered.

'Hello, Joanne. I wanted to ask you about Derek,' I got in quickly when she paused for breath. 'Has his condition improved?'

I could hear the sorrow in her voice when she replied. 'No, Felicity. There's been no improvement. His condition was terrible before John tried to kill him. It's a miracle he survived the fall. How he got away without broken bones I will never know.'

'Is he still unconscious?' I wanted to know.

A small sob and sniff came over the phone. 'Yes. They sound hopeful, but I just don't want to give myself too much hope. What if he never wakes up?' she wailed.

Regretfully, I knew exactly how she felt. Archie faded fast after his diagnosis. He'd been putting off going to see a doctor because he was

101

sure the pain he felt would turn out to be nothing. It wasn't, and by the time he finally sought help, it was too late for them to do anything.

I wouldn't wish the same experience on anyone. All I could do was make appropriate noises of sympathy and tell her to hope for the best. Given the state Derek was in prior to his 'accident' a pragmatist would argue it might be better to prepare for the worst.

When it felt appropriate to do so, I said, 'You probably don't know this, but I ran into John last night when I went out for dinner. He sort of threatened me …' Joanne gasped, but I ploughed on, 'and he said he wasn't the crook at the firm. Have you got any idea what he meant by that?'

I suspected it was a dodgy question to ask. If Joanne knew something and it did tie to Derek, I doubted she would tell me anything. If it didn't tie to Derek, I doubted she would know – she didn't work at the firm.

Joanne repeated my words. 'A crook at the firm?'

'That's what John said.'

'No, sorry, Felicity. I don't know anything about that. Derek rarely talked to me about the print business. He knew I found it boring. You could ask Tamara. Or Tarquin,' she added with a suggestion of enthusiasm to her tone. It made me think she must really like her daughter's choice of husband. 'Tarquin is essentially running the place anyway.' Her voice turned glum again and she murmured. 'Especially with both Derek and now John out of the picture.'

We talked for a few more seconds. I got on okay with Joanne, but I was friends with Derek and didn't really know his wife.

With the call ended, I finally got myself ready for the day. Selecting a black skirt and a pure white blouse, I paired it with black knee-length boots and a camel brown rainmac. I popped my Prada sunglasses on my face, hooked my handbag over my left arm, and went in search of Amber.

She has several favoured spots in my house, all of which are deliberately out of reach of Buster so he couldn't mess with her while she slept. That didn't stop him from sneaking up for a surprise bark attack when he felt she might not be expecting it, but today I found her on the windowsill in my bedroom, asleep and alone.

She opened a suspicious eye as I approached.

'You really want to go through with this?' she asked.

'You really want a poached mackerel?' Before she could reply, I scooped her up and onto my chest where she dug her claws in to hold on. Mercifully, the rainmac bore the brunt of her assault, but I felt the tiny daggers find my skin in several places even with it to protect me.

I needed to take Buster and Amber out at the same time and putting them in the front seat of my sports car at the same time would be much like putting them, and me, in a tumble dryer. It was for that reason that we were taking my other car.

Having two cars when I am a widow who lives alone might seem completely redundant and I would not argue. However, I didn't buy the second car, it was Archie's pride and joy. When he passed, I kept it.

My husband had been something of a car nut. Not that he lived in the garage and could be found forever tinkering under the bonnet, but he knew his cars and had rebuilt the mark two Ford Escort Mexico all by himself. It took him three years. I remember feeling entirely nonplussed when he brought it home … on a trailer because it didn't run.

However, when it was finished, even though it wasn't my kind of car, I had to admit that there was a certain something about it. Now considered a modern classic, the late 1970s car was what I used when my two-seater Mercedes was an impractical choice.

Today was such a day.

Amber was less than happy. *'Why am I the one going in the travel cage!'* she raged, clawing at the edges as I tried to slide her into it.

'Because Buster doesn't fit,' I explained through gritted teeth. I really needed a pair of those gloves they use to handle barbed wire. 'And if he did, I wouldn't be able to carry him.'

Snagging the last paw still hooked around a bar, I stuffed it inside and closed the plastic cage door. From inside came several unrepeatable phrases. One was to do with a dead pigeon and where she would like to put it – there had been no mention of lubricant.

Trotting happily over, Buster sniffed at Amber's cage where I'd set it on the carpet.

'Oh, yes,' he commented. *'This is much more like it.'*

Amber screeched, *'Felicity!'*

Just in time, I flicked out a toe to nudge his back leg. He was manoeuvring himself into position.

'Buster! Don't you dare!'

He spun around looking surprised. *'I've no idea what you are talking about.'*

I wagged a finger at him as I checked I had everything. 'You were going to widdle on the cage with Amber in it. Don't you tell me you weren't.'

Grumbling at being thwarted, he trotted to the door and waited there for me to catch up.

I got them to the garage, got Archie's old car warmed up and ready to go, and set off for my boutique in Rochester.

My agenda for the day was filling fast and it had been full before I started to add in additional tasks like solving a crime.

I went the long route, sweeping out through Cuxton and Halling, turning left at the new bridge to cross the river by Peter's Village. I needed to get back to Aylesford; the scene of the crime, you might say.

It was already after my usual time to arrive at work when I pulled up behind Orion Print again so I paused to call Justin – Archie's old car has no handsfree system.

'Felicity,' Justin blurted. 'Mindy just arrived with the wildest story.'

'It's true,' I cut him off before he could say anything else. 'I got arrested last night and released this morning. I'm running a little late, but I'll be there in about half an hour. I was just calling to let you know.'

'Are you okay?' he asked.

I replied with, 'I'll be fine.' It wasn't a lie. At least I didn't think it was. Nothing really terrible had happened. In fact, looking back at it, the worst part was being spotted by Primrose. I was lucky Vince came along or she might have had pictures of me all over social media by now. I wouldn't put it past her to email the people in my supply chain anyway and felt certain she would do her best to make sure prospective clients found out about my arrest.

Thinking about the potential damage she might do steeled my will to solve the mystery and clear my name.

Shaking my head to clear it and refocus on what I was doing, I said, 'I'll be there soon, Justin. I have to meet with the Couture Bridal Designs at noon and have quite a bit to do before then.'

'I can take some more on,' Justin swiftly volunteered. 'Mindy can help out too,' he added.

I was sure she could. I ended the call and placed my phone back into my handbag.

'Ready, Amber?' I asked. 'Ready to earn a mackerel?'

'*This is demeaning,*' she growled from the cage.

'Which bit?' I enquired, unsure exactly what she might be unhappy about.

'*Helping out,*' she replied snippily. '*I'm a cat. I'm here to be worshipped. Doing things is not what cats do.*'

Sensing that she was just sounding off, I confirmed, 'But you'll do it for a mackerel?'

'*It had better be a big one.*'

I had to get out of the car to be able to get her cage from the back seat. I set it on the tarmac of the carpark and opened the little door.

Lazily, languidly, she sauntered out; Amber was never one to hurry. My ragdoll cat performed a stretch, making her body seem twice the length it had been, then sat and started to clean a paw.

'I'll come back to this spot,' I told her. 'Just remember what I need you to do.'

'*Yes, yes,*' she replied. '*It's all very easy. Take the mutt and enjoy your day. If you feel like leaving him somewhere, I will take that in reward over a fish any day of the week.*'

Buster barked an insult of his own in response but couldn't get to the cat when he lunged because he was strapped to the passenger seat. The dog harness let him get his front paws on to the driver's seat before arresting his movement. At that point, he flipped and landed on his back. Now turned turtle on the passenger seat, his little paws waved helplessly in the air.

Amber tutted and walked away.

Righting himself, Buster said, '*Quick, let's go! She'll never find us if we pack up and move home today.*'

'We are coming back for her later,' I assured him.

Buster licked his nose. '*There's just no cure for what you have, is there?*'

Given that I was having a conversation with my dog, I worried he might be right. As I pulled away, I wound down my window to call to Amber, but she was already nowhere in sight. Wondering if I was a genius or an idiot, and certain I would find out in the next day or so, I pointed the car towards Rochester and enjoyed working the stick as I took the back roads through the countryside to get there.

Too Distracted

There was a coffee waiting for me when I arrived; I could see it through the front window of the boutique. No doubt Mindy made the trip to the coffee shop in the High Street because it was one of the few tasks she knew how to do and because Justin felt prompted by my phone call.

Justin jumped to his feet when he spotted me coming in. 'Felicity, goodness, I still can't believe something like this would happen to you.'

Mindy appeared from the backroom with a stack of promotional material in her hands. 'Oh, hi, Auntie. How was the big house?'

The juxtaposition in attitude felt like social commentary on the generational gap. Justin was horrified to hear I got arrested. Mindy thought it was cool.

Opting to focus on my business, I said, 'It's something we can discuss at a later date. Right now, we have several weddings looming and a need to fill our diary as far into next year as we can.' Justin knew how right I was. Our continued success depended entirely upon landing the next big client and the one after that, ad infinitum. One thing with our market was the lack of repeat custom.

It happened sometimes that an attendee at one of our weddings would then be impressed enough to choose my firm without even looking for alternatives, but for the most part I was out hunting down the clients, not waiting for them to come to me.

For the weddings already booked and being arranged there were all manner of strange and wonderful requests. We had a request to get Rod Stewart to perform at a billionaire octogenarian's wedding. He was tying the knot with an athletic woman in her early thirties. My biggest hope with that wedding was that the groom would survive to attend the ceremony. Trying to book Rod Stewart is just one example of where my time goes.

Not that I mind. Weddings like that one would pay all our wages and all the bills for the year and do me no harm in my bid to attract the attention of Prince Markus.

We settled down to get to work and I tried to focus my attention, I truly did. The wedding on Raven Island next weekend would see me and my entire entourage travelling to stay there on Friday. Justin was going two days earlier with Mindy to start making sure everything was as it should be. They would be there to meet the caterers as they arrived, oversee cleaning, make arrangements for the band who were to arrive on the Saturday morning … there was a lot to do. The celebrity couple had spent over forty thousand pounds just on flowers which all had to be arranged according to their specifications.

To make things more interesting, the island could only be accessed by vehicle twice a day at low tide. There was a window of about forty minutes when the causeway became exposed, that is provided a storm hadn't shifted a sandbar to make it impassable or it wasn't the time of the moon cycle when the low tide was still too high to expose the road.

Complex? Yes. That's why they pay me the big bucks.

Yet, despite all that stuff swirling around in my head, I could not shift the questions about Derek Bleakwith and John Ramsey. Who was the man I overheard plotting to destroy evidence last night? Who did tamper with John Ramsey's brakes? It certainly wasn't Derek getting his own back for John pushing him. Were they even tampered with? Or had Vince, the pirate that he is, made it up because he wanted to come to my house for breakfast?

After an hour of not being very productive because I just couldn't get my mind to stay on the job, I accepted defeat.

'Mindy do you feel like getting out of the boutique for a while? I need to visit a few people.'

My question made Justin raise his head. 'Everything okay, Felicity?'

I gave him a half shrug and blew out a breath to show my frustration. 'I am distracted by the events of last night,' I told him the truth. 'I can't concentrate so I'm going to feed the voices in my head and hope they shut up.'

Mindy asked, 'What are you going to feed them with?' She had a hopeful expression like I was going to take her out for burgers.

With a deep breath in through my nose, I set my resolve and said, 'Answers.'

Buster clambered to his feet, licking his nose with a snuffling snort. *'Adventure dog reporting for duty. Let's go get the bad guys.'*

I collected my coat and bag, gave Buster's lead to Mindy – she could strain to keep him under control instead of me for once – and we left the boutique.

In the carpark, Mindy spotted Archie's car. 'Oh, wow! I didn't realise you still had this. Uncle Archibald's car is soooo old. How come you have this and not your Mercedes?'

I frowned but said nothing. The car wasn't as old as me. I opened my mouth to explain that I'd needed to drop Amber off this morning but shut it again before the first word made it past my lips. How would I explain deploying a feline spy to anyone?

Instead, I lied. 'I fancied a change, and it does it good to have a run every now and then. Otherwise, things start to seize.' Don't ask me where I dredged that little snippet of information from. I expect it was something Archie once said.

Mindy grabbed the passenger door handle and tried to open it. She expected central locking, of course. The idea of a car that had to be opened with a key one door at a time was completely alien to her. This was probably like travelling back in time.

I had to coax Buster into the back and fiddle with the seat belt again to make sure he was secure.

He said, '*I'm sure the official sidekick needs to ride shotgun.*'

Tightening his harness, I whispered. 'You'll be more comfortable back here. There's plenty of room for you to stretch out.'

'*More like limber up,*' he grunted. '*I need my muscles loose if I am to fight criminals and deliver justice this day.*'

I really need to start unplugging the television before I leave him in the house.

Mindy was in the front seat and all buckled in when I finally settled behind the wheel. Her eyes were agog as she looked around the vintage car.

'It's so sparse,' she commented. 'It doesn't come with any extras at all.' She gasped as her eyes stopped at the stereo. 'Oh, my goodness. That looks like it came off the Ark! What is that slot for?'

'Cassettes.'

'What now?' She was poking the hole a cassette would go in with one delicate fingernail.

I chuckled at her and turned the key, keen to get going.

Nothing happened. Pulling a face, I tried again.

I got the same result and said a rude word. There were no lights on the dashboard. Not a thing. The car didn't even click when I turned the key.

'Something wrong?' asked Mindy.

Huffing, I unclipped my seatbelt again. 'The car won't start. I'm going to look under the bonnet.'

Two minutes later, Mindy and I were both staring at what I thought was the engine. I could identify the battery and the radiator. It got a bit murky after that.

'We could take my car,' Mindy suggested.

It honestly hadn't occurred to me.

With the bonnet of the Escort shut again, all the doors locked, and Buster transferred between cars, we eventually set off just a few minutes later.

Mindy drives a new plate Renault Clio Williams Supersport and when I say she drives it, what I mean is she uses it as a tool to test the planet's gravitational pull. Ever seen *The Italian Job*? Our journey to Maidstone Hospital was like that only much, much scarier.

On the backseat, Buster was loving it. '*Yeah, this is how we should drive all the time!*' he slobbered behind my ear. '*Tell her to press the button that makes the machine guns pop out of the bonnet.*'

I seriously doubted Mindy's car had those, but I wasn't going to ask … you know, just in case. She'd already shocked me to my core recently by revealing herself to be some kind of ninja. Today, she was wearing an elegant pencil skirt and heels with a satin top and an office appropriate winter coat, but I would not be surprised to learn she had a short sword strapped between her shoulder blades or some throwing stars in her handbag.

'Have you always driven like this?' I asked her, gripping the handle above my head until my knuckles turned white.

She shot me a grin. 'It's like you said about giving them a run sometimes. The route through the towns will be terrible at this time of day but the back roads through the countryside are empty.'

She was right and I often picked them for the same reason. However, when I came this way, I didn't attempt to break the land speed record.

In the next second, she crested a small rise and the land dropped away more quickly than inertia would allow the car to follow. We were momentarily airborne, which made my stomach rebel and caused Buster to whoop with joy.

When the wheels touched down, and once I was sure I wasn't about to be sick, I asked, 'Can you slow it down a little, please?'

Mindy grinned again. 'Sure thing, Auntie.' Her pace slowed, and as it did, she said, 'I wanted to take up rally driving. Dad bought me one of those experience days for my eighteenth, but mum said it was not a thing for a lady to do. I like going fast.'

I had no doubt about that.

We got to Maidstone Hospital a good deal quicker than we would have had I been behind the wheel and found a parking space straight away for once.

Buster couldn't go in, but Mindy had spotted a sandwich joint across the street and volunteered to walk him. Like a lot of teenagers, she was eternally hungry and never seemed to gain any weight. She probably had the same genetic characteristic that kept my sister and I so skinny. Ginny is taller than me by several inches, but otherwise we look quite similar and though she had a child, her hips remained as narrow as ever.

Inside the hospital, two ladies on the reception desk were able to point me in the right direction for Derek Bleakwith. He was in the critical care ward which I guessed was at least one rung down from intensive care.

Arriving on the ward, I heard the commotion before I saw it.

'This is what he needs,' insisted a woman whose voice was familiar to my ears. 'He's been prescribed this cream for months now and he had been improving.'

'But that's just topical corticosteroid cream,' argued a man in calm tones.

I reached the door to Derek's room and looked inside. Joanne Bleakwith was facing off against a young man wearing a blue oxford shirt and fitted grey chinos. I could see identification clipped to his left breast pocket and though I could not see what it said, he looked and spoke like a doctor. Standing to his side was an attractive woman of about the same age. She was dressed similarly but in a ladies' version of the same clothes. She also had a badge stuck to her shirt.

In the corner behind Joanne, a middle-aged woman in a nurse's uniform failed to keep the disapproving glare from her features. It was aimed at Joanne.

'I want him to have this cream. I will administer it myself,' Joanne insisted. She sounded close to hysterical.

The man was trying to be sympathetic to her concerns but wasn't budging. 'Mrs Bleakwith, I cannot allow that. Your husband's condition will be treated according to my instructions. There is no need for you to worry. The cream you are holding is exactly what the nurses here are applying twice daily.'

'That's what I already told her,' claimed the nurse in the corner, speaking for the first time since I arrived. Her expression was savage, not helped by a face that only a mother could love. 'She kept saying her cream was the right stuff and that it was a new tub she picked up this

115

morning.' That she had been arguing with Joanne before the doctors arrived was clear in the nurse's exasperated tone.

The male doctor offered Joanne kindly eyes. 'Nurse Growler is a respected member of the team, Mrs Bleakwith. Her team will ensure your husband is given the right treatment.'

As if his calm demeanour was the flame lighting her fuse, Joanne exploded. 'NO! I want him to have what *his* doctor prescribed. He has been under the personal care of Dr Kimble for more than a year now. If you start messing with his treatment, you'll set him back months.' She was close to tears.

I wanted to say something. Hovering in the doorway as I was, I felt like I was eavesdropping, but there was no lull in their conversation.

The doctor went to Derek's bedside. 'Mrs Bleakwith, I have discussed your husband's condition with several of my colleagues and a leading dermatology consultant. No one can explain why his condition is as bad as it is, but I can assure you, we will get him better. The injuries from his fall are superficial and he could wake up at any time. I know the police will be keen to speak with him when he does.'

Joanne sobbed, still clutching the large tub of cream as if it were the only thing keeping her afloat. 'I just want him to get better and come home. This whole thing with his skin and his joints has been such a nightmare. You really think you can find a cure?'

The young doctor reached across to place a comforting hand on Joanne's shoulder. 'We have a biopsy of his skin for testing. Your husband's condition appears to be nothing but a really bad case of dermatitis, one that ought to have been cleared up with the cream you have so diligently been applying. However, we are checking to be certain there is nothing more sinister attacking his skin and will have an answer in a few hours. As for his joints, that looks to be an acute case of bursitis. We can treat that too, but first we must determine what is causing it. The symptoms are most unusual both in their severity and their presentation.'

Joanne's head was down, her eyes closed as she fought her misery.

Using the hand still on her shoulder, the doctor steered Joanne back toward the door and they finally spotted me standing there.

As if the sight of me were the catalyst, the dam holding back Joanne's tears finally burst and they came forth, her shoulders shaking as sobs racked her body. The young doctor stepped away as I stepped in.

Putting an arm around her shoulders, I did my best to try to soothe her. 'He's going to be all right, Joanne. That's what the doctors said. You just need to give it time.'

'It's all been so awful, Felicity,' Joanne cried into me. I was taking her weight on my shoulder, my head turned to the side which gave me a view of Derek.

I remembered him as a little boy at school. Best friends with John Ramsey despite how John treated me. His face, indeed all the parts of his skin that I could see, were red and blotchy and there were open sores visible. He looked a terrible state. No wonder Joanne was so worked up about it.

I gave her some time to weep, staying quiet until she got her breathing under control again. As I expected, she broke the embrace we were in, pushing away and embarrassed by her public display of emotion. In moving, her scarf came free, floating to the floor.

As I bent to pick it up for her, she said, 'Goodness, I must look such a mess,' she dabbed at her eyes with a tissue. Meeting my eyes, she said, 'I'm so sorry, Felicity.'

I waved off her apology. 'It's perfectly all right.' I could remember how unable to control my emotions I had been in the weeks following Archie's death. 'Here.' I offered her the scarf, holding it out for her. When she took it, I said, 'That goes with your outfit really well, did you get it somewhere local?' I was just trying to say something nice and offering an opportunity to change the subject.

She took the offered accessory and stuffed it into a coat pocket without commenting or thanking me. Then, her expression changed as a question suddenly occurred to her. 'Did you come here to see Derek?' she asked.

Now on the spot, I found myself questioning why I had come to the hospital. I was snooping, that was the truth of it, trying to engage my inner Patricia Fisher, if I had such a thing. Cringingly, I had no idea what I was doing, or even ought to do. Would I know a clue if I fell over it?

Needing to give Joanne an answer, I said, 'I feel a little lost, is all. I'm sure you heard I was arrested last night after John Ramsey crashed his car.'

Joanne gasped, her jaw dropping open. 'No, I had no idea. Why did they arrest you?'

Now I had to tell her the truth of it, taking a few moments to describe the circumstances that led me to be outside her husband's printing business last night, spotting John's car and the need I felt to look in it. Amazingly for me, I managed to not reveal my breaking and entering crime, leaving her to believe the police thought it was me because they saw me vanish into the shadows by the car on the carpark CCTV camera.

'But they let you go?' Joanne sought to confirm.

'I have a good lawyer.' I didn't expand on my statement.

Joanne looked down at the large tub of topical corticosteroid cream in her left hand. The size of a half-litre tub of ice cream, it looked new but the plastic tab that would indicate it had never been opened was broken off. Nurse Growler continued to eye Joanne with suspicion. If Joanne had a plan to defy the doctors and apply the cream she held anyway, she would have to subdue the guard dog nurse they left behind first.

Joanne twisted around to look at Nurse Growler. Her lips twitched as if she wanted to say something, but ultimately decided against it.

Doing my best to help the situation while staying completely neutral, I said, 'The doctors think he will regain consciousness soon. Maybe he will be home in a day or so and you can continue his treatment then.'

Discontent, but accepting that she had no choice, Joanne nodded her head. It was a sad little motion that came without words. Still holding the tub of cream, she crossed the room to kiss Derek on the top of his head – one of the few places his skin wasn't breaking out – then left the room.

I had to chase after her to catch up.

Still playing sleuth, I asked what I hoped would sound like an innocent question. 'Where's Tamara today?'

Joanne was fishing in her bag, her hand chasing keys around until she found them. 'Tamara had other things to do,' she replied a little snippily.

'More important than visiting her father?' I hadn't meant for my response to sound so judgemental, but that was how it came out.

Joanne frowned at me. 'We are not all rich wedding planners, Felicity.'

Automatically, I apologised, 'I'm sorry, Joanne. That came out wrong.'

Joanne, barrelled on as if I hadn't spoken, in many ways reminding me that it was Derek I was friends with and not her. 'Tamara went to work today. The printing business won't run itself, and with John gone,' she stopped talking to take a shuddering breath. 'Well, we need to keep the ship afloat. There are orders to meet and someone has to keep the staff employed.'

Should I tell her about the man I heard talking last night? The question argued back and forth in my head as we made our way back toward the front entrance to the hospital. In the end, I ran out of time as Joanne pointed her key fob at a sleek black Audi.

Stopping so abruptly I carried on a pace before I realised she was no longer with me, I turned to face her.

'I appreciate you coming to visit Derek today, Felicity, and I know you need to meet with us again to set diary dates for cake tasting and dress fitting among other things. But can it wait a week, please? I think Tamara and I both need to focus our efforts on Derek and the business.'

There was no way I could impose myself on them. If they wanted to push back my meetings, they were my clients after all, not the other way around.

Mindy was coming back across the carpark, Buster tugging at her arm the whole time. She shot me a wave when she saw me look her way.

Joanne backed toward her car, saying, 'I really must go.'

I turned my head to ask her to call me when she and Tamara were ready to discuss the wedding plans again, but she was already closing the car door.

I watched her pull away, wondering how she might cope if Derek's condition continued to worsen. It was a horrible thought, but of course, that was what had driven Tamara and Tarquin to bring their wedding plans forward. I only hoped I could deliver what they wanted in the reduced timescale and had to question if Derek would even be able to attend.

But here's a thing about being a sleuth - not that I knew it yet – you might see a clue at any point but not know what it was until much later. I had just seen something on Joanne's car which at this point meant nothing at all.

Reeling Buster in when she got to me, Mindy asked. 'Did you learn anything, Auntie?'

I shook my head. 'No, I don't think so. Derek ... that's my friend,' I explained, 'is still unconscious.' Her question caused me to think about what it was that I was trying to achieve. 'Let's get in the car,' I suggested, wanting to keep our conversation private because I had decided to tell Mindy a little more about last night.

'Where to?' Mindy asked, her finger poised over the big red start button.

It was a great question. My list of suspects for John Ramsey's murder had zero entries. Like the chief inspector said, I was the one who didn't like him and wanted to see him fall. John tried to kill Derek, but who tried to kill John, and what was any of it about? John was upset about Derek trying to run the business from his sickbed. It still seemed a stretch that he might wish to kill Derek for it. Although Derek's death would resolve the issue and leave John in a position to appoint Tarquin.

Hold on though. Joanne said Tarquin was effectively running the firm anyway, so what did it matter to John if Tarquin was officially appointed to the role of CEO or not?

I didn't know the answer but a trip to Orion Print's office would allow me to ask some questions. Nodding to myself, I said, 'Mindy, let's go to Aylesford.'

Mindy parked her car in the exact same spot mine had inhabited last night. I felt like I had crammed a lot into the last twenty-four hours. Getting out of her car, I started calling for my cat.

'Amber. Amber are you here?'

Mindy asked with a frown. 'Why would Amber be here? You live miles away.'

Oh. How was I going to explain this? Quickly thinking up a lie, I said, 'I thought I saw her, is all. It must have been another ragdoll cat though.'

Mindy raised her eyebrows but said nothing, probably thinking her aunt was going a little loopy.

Unlike last night, I walked around to the front of the building and went in through the customer entrance.

An exuberant young man bounced away from a display he was tidying to greet us both. 'Hello. Welcome to Orion Print. My name is Graham Mailer, I'm one of the sales reps. Is there something specific we can help you with today?'

I shook his hand, noting the man's dainty grip. 'I'm Felicity Philips. This is my niece, Mindy.'

Mindy got a polite nod from the employee who then cast his eyes down to look at Buster.

Buster's tongue snuck out to give his nose a lick before slithering noisily back into his mouth again.

'Wow, a bulldog. I don't remember the last time I saw one of these. He's so cute.'

123

'*Cute?*' sneered Buster. '*I am darkness and vengeance. I am what you fear in the shadows.*' He lunged forward before I could stop him and tried to bite the man's foot.

Dancing back to stay out of reach, the man gave a nervous laugh to cover up the unmanly squeal of fright Mindy and I both heard. 'He's a little feisty.'

I was about to explain that I got all my printing done here and was a very minor co-owner. I didn't need to though because Tamara appeared.

'Oh, hi, Felicity,' she smiled at me as she came through from the office I was in last night. 'It's so good of you to come to me.'

A little lost for words but guessing she believed I was here to pick up where we left off yesterday, I said, 'Of course. My clients get the best treatment, even if they are the daughters of my friends. We all want your big day to be as special as it can be. I just popped in to rearrange a few things with you.'

Mindy shot me a confused look. 'I thought we were …'

Shutting her up as quickly as I could, I said, 'That's why we came, Mindy. Tamara is going to be one of our fabulous brides.'

Still looking confused, Mindy said, 'Okay,' and gave Tamara the professional smile I'd been teaching her.

'We never did get to discuss the dress yesterday, did we,' I gave her my most excited eyes. If there is one thing I know for absolute certain: every bride on the planet wants her wedding dress to be amazing. If you can sell a client on the dress, the rest of it is easy.

Tamara's eyes were alight with excitement.

I took my tablet from my bag and handed it to Mindy. I wanted her to feel useful even if this was a task I could easily do for myself.

'When do you want to visit the dress shops and when can we schedule a proper discussion about your dress?' The salesrep, seeing that he need play no part in our conversation, drifted back to the display he'd been working on when we arrived. 'I have several shops at my disposal, all of which will give you a private appointment. We'll need to schedule in half a day for each one we plan to visit, which is why we have the meeting to discuss your desires first. That way we can narrow it down and hopefully find what you want more quickly. We are pushed for time, after all.'

'Why the hurry?' asked Mindy. 'You don't look like you're up the duff.'

I closed my eyes in abject horror just as Tamara gave my assistant a surprised expression.

'I'm not,' the bride-to-be choked out, 'thank you very much.'

Pinching the bridge of my nose between thumb and forefinger, I swivelled on my heels to face Mindy. I found myself wishing it were twenty years ago when I carried a clipboard and bits of paper. I could have whacked her over the head with it and not felt too bad.

'Mindy, we do not question our clients about their motivations. Ever,' I added. 'We most certainly do not ask them if they are up the duff.' I was growling by the end of the sentence.

Mindy at least had the sense to look embarrassed. 'Sorry?' she tried. I bugged my eyes out and flicked them in the direction of our bride to be. 'Sorry,' Mindy addressed her apology to Tamara this time.

Tamara accepted it with a nod. 'If you must know, my dad has been really ill. I begged Tarquin to bring the date forward so dad might still be well enough to walk me down the aisle.' She skewed her lips to one side, thinking private thoughts before adding, 'I guess I thought we were going to lose him.'

'I ran into your mother at the hospital,' I told her, thinking Tamara probably didn't know. The doctors seem quite confident that he will regain consciousness soon.'

Tamara brightened. 'I know. I went there first thing before I came to work. They said his skin is improving too.'

'They did?' I questioned her without thinking.

She nodded her head vigorously. 'There was a consultant in his room when I got there. Some old guy in his fifties.' I refused to react to her comment about age or point out that I am already in my late fifties. 'He said he couldn't work out why dad's skin was so bad. He said it was just dermatitis. The worst case he had ever seen, but just dermatitis. He said much the same about his joint pain and made it sound like Doctor Kimble had failed to provide proper care for dad. Not that he said those words,' she added. 'Do you think he might get better?' she asked me.

How was I supposed to answer that? I went with a non-committal, 'God willing.' I said the words, but my brain was elsewhere. Derek was getting better. He'd only been in hospital overnight and his condition was already improving. That meant something. It had to. Now I had to try to work out what.

Tamara looked into the middle distance for a moment, a thoughtful expression on her face. Then she shook her head as if trying to rid it of whatever images might have been plaguing it and looked at me with a smile.

'When can you fit me in?' she asked. 'For the dress consultation, I mean.'

I allowed myself a small chuckle. 'You have that about face, Tamara. It is I who wish to know when you can fit me in. You are the bride; this is all about you. However, I will say that we should attempt to get together soon. In the next day or so ideally, so I can make arrangements with the establishments that will best suit your needs.'

'Oh,' Tamara made a concerned face. 'Well, I really need to commit to work at the moment.' She made a pained face, and her lip began to wobble unexpectantly. The next second, far too fast for me to be able to react, her face folded in on itself and she started crying.

Mindy's eyes went as wide as saucers and she backed away just as I went forward.

'I'm sorry,' Tamara sobbed as she stepped forward into my embrace. 'It's so strange being here without John. I just … I just can't believe he's gone. I know he might have hurt dad, but now John's dead and …' Whatever she planned to say next got lost as emotions she'd been keeping in check spilled out in a torrent.

For the next minute, I did nothing but hold the young woman upright. She leaned into me; a head taller but in need of my support as I became the rock she could anchor to. Just like I had with Joanne a few hours ago, I soaked up the tears and waited for her self-control to return.

When she was ready, Tamara started to apologise again, pushing herself away to get out of my personal space. She exhaled deeply as she tried to rid herself of the shudders her tearful fit left behind.

'Oh, goodness,' she sniffed and blew her nose. 'I don't even like John. He was never very nice to work with. It was always business, business,

business with him. I'm sorry,' she said for the fourth or fifth time. 'You probably have other things you need to do.'

I did, but I wasn't going to say that. Remembering my conversation with Joanne, I thought about what I came here to find out. I wasn't going to ask Tamara about crooks in the business though. Not given her delicate emotional state.

Instead, I asked, 'Is Tarquin here? I have a few groom-related questions for him.'

Tamara shook her head. 'No, sorry. He went to London first thing this morning. He's trying to land a new big client.'

I sucked on my teeth for a second while I weighed up my options and glanced around for any sign of Amber. I expected to see her sitting on top of a filing cabinet somewhere inside the office, but if she was here, she was hiding well.

A tinge of worry lit in my core.

Tamara was waiting for me to say something and making it clear with her body language that she felt a need to get on with other things.

'We should get out of your hair,' I announced, but as I did so a fresh option occurred to me. 'We could schedule your dress discussion for before or after office hours if that helps. I can fit you in this evening.'

Tamara's beamed with excitement. It was like watching a bulb get switched on inside her face. Then the smile fell as if the bulb had just blown.

'I can't. I'm having dinner with Tarquin tonight,' she explained.

Undeterred, I tried again. 'How about tomorrow?'

The bride-to-be cast her eyes skyward, checked her mental diary. Then the smile returned.

'Sure. Does six o'clock work?' she asked. 'I can come straight to you from here when I finish work.'

I confirmed that was fine by me, had Mindy make an entry in my diary, and finally let Tamara get back to work.

Back at the car, I had another scout around for Amber. I knew I shouldn't worry; cats are so independent and Amber especially so. I really didn't like not knowing where she was though.

Mindy plipped the car open so I could get in and folded the driver's seat forward so Buster could clamber through to the back seat. Once the doors were closed, I started talking.

'I think John might have been tampering with Derek's medication.'

Mindy had a finger half an inch from the car's start button and a thoughtful expression on her face.

'You mean like swapping it for something else or adding something to it? Do you think that is why his skin was so bad and not getting any better?'

I pursed my lips, checking my thoughts. John went to the house all the time. Derek's condition probably started naturally enough, but John could have added something to the cream at any point. Joanne would have been diligently applying it to her husband unaware that she was the one making his skin worse.

'I think we need to go to John's house,' I murmured as much to myself as it was to Mindy.

Mindy tilted her head. 'To do more snooping?' She sounded excited at the prospect.

I didn't want to call it snooping, but what other word could I come up with?

'More like investigating,' I tried. 'I doubt we will find anything, but maybe there will be a clue in his trash.'

'His trash?' Mindy made a disgusted face.

I'd seen detective shows where they went through a suspect's rubbish to find vital clues. Maybe that would work for me too. Would he shred his paper waste? Remembering the pages I took from John's car, I had to wonder if there might be more in his trash. They were important enough for him to have scribbled notes on with lots of exclamation marks.

I nodded to myself. 'It's bin day tomorrow. We have one chance to see if there is anything to find. There is something going on at Orion Print. Something that made John want to kill Derek and in turn got John killed.'

Mindy's eyebrows bunched together. 'I thought his brakes failed due to poor maintenance?' she questioned. 'Wasn't that what you said earlier? That's why the police let you go.'

'It was. You are right. I also heard a different story. Vince,' Mindy knew him from the previous weekend at Loxton Hall, 'said it was more likely the brakes were tampered with. Also, I ... um. I sort of broke into their office last night and overheard a man talking about destroying evidence.'

Mindy was gaping at me. 'Auntie, you are a total badass! You broke in!'

My cheeks went red. Even if Mindy did think I was cool, criminal activity was not something I wanted to endorse or be praised for.

'Well, in truth, Vince broke in and I went with him. Look, the point is I am sure someone has been up to something and I think John discovered it. His car crashing like that is just too much coincidence. The more I think about it, the less willing I am to believe it was an accident.'

Mindy stabbed the start button with a determined finger and the engine roared to life. 'Right then, Auntie. Where to?'

John Ramsey was a life-long bachelor so there was no danger of finding his grieving widow at home. His lack of family was one of the things that made him so good at his job, but also so hard to work with, I suspected. He had no distractions. His work was his life and while it could be said that he'd done well as a businessman, no job will ever love you back. I imagined he had an empty life outside of work.

Finding his address was easy enough, I looked it up on Companies House where my own address is also listed as a minor shareholder.

Mindy needed to use the motorway to get there, which allowed her to once again see if she could accelerate off the side of the planet. It wasn't so much the top speed she achieved, which was over the seventy limit, though not by a scary amount, but more the rate at which she got there.

'Mindy, please slow down,' I begged as she swung around a truck and floored the pedal yet again.

She flicked a glance in her rear-view mirror. She'd been doing it a lot recently.

'Auntie, I think we are being followed.'

'Don't be daft,' I countered without giving any credence to her claim. 'Why would anyone be following us?'

'I'm not making it up, Auntie,' Mindy argued, her eyes checking the rear-view again. 'There's a black BMW back there and it's been behind me since we left Aylesford. I think I saw it before that too.'

'Go faster, see if you can lose it,' barked Buster. I pretended I hadn't heard him.

Twisting in my seat, I craned my neck to get a look back down the motorway.

'Don't look, Auntie! He'll know we are onto him if he sees you looking.'

'You're just being paranoid,' I replied, hoping I was right.

'*I bet it's the killer,*' said Buster. '*He knows you're onto him and he's worried my alter ego, Adventure Dog, will track him down and beat him to a pulp so the police can arrest him.*'

'Is Buster all right?' asked Mindy, sounding worried. 'He doesn't need to go potty, does he?'

I ignored them both for a second, staring at the black BMW. It was thirty yards behind, steadily tracking us, but the same could be said for the car behind that and the car behind that. We were on a three-lane motorway so all the cars were going in the same direction at more or less the same speed.

'I'm going to try something,' Mindy announced.

I got enough warning to form a sentence asking what she had in mind, but not enough time to pose it.

My niece cranked the steering wheel to the right, swung out to pass an articulated truck while simultaneously blasting her car from seventy miles per hour to over a hundred in the blink of an eye.

'*Yeaaahhhh!*' whooped Buster. Pressed back into my seat I flicked my eyes around to look at him. You know how people look when they are subjected to extremes of gravity and their skin all pulls backward away from their face? Well, Buster looks like that all the time. Even so, he was also pressed back into his seat but unlike me he was loving it.

Mindy came past the lorry, gave her rear-view a quick check, and shouted, 'Hold on to something!'

What? What was I supposed to hold onto? A bible? A cherished picture of Archie so they could find it clutched to my dead chest?

The moment she was clear of the truck, she threw the wheel hard left and I saw what she had in mind. To a blast of deep bass horn from the truck driver, she crossed all three lanes and shot down an off ramp. It wasn't the exit we wanted, but the black BMW shot by and whether the driver had been following us or not, he certainly wasn't now.

I drew a breath and relaxed my jaw when pain from it told me I'd been clenching my teeth.

Mindy was smiling. 'That got rid of him.'

With eyes like saucers, I tried to get my pulse back under control. 'How do you know it was a man driving?' I asked her. I hadn't been able to see anything other than an indistinct figure through the tinted screen.

Mindy shrugged. 'He drove like a man?' she hazarded. 'You think maybe it was a woman?'

I was still far from convinced we'd been getting followed at all, but I didn't have the energy to argue.

'Let's just stick to country roads now,' I suggested. 'And please drive sedately. I'm not sure how much more of your adventurous driving my heart can take.'

The rest of the journey was conducted at a pace I felt happy with though I was still glad to get out of the car when she pulled it to a stop.

John Ramsey's house is in the small village of Godsmersham not far from the city of Ashford where the Eurostar train makes its final stop before crossing to France through the tunnel. He owned a modest semi-detached place that was neither cherished nor abandoned. The two-story structure needed a lick of paint on both the masonry and the window frames. The roof showed several broken tiles and the guttering and soffits had seen better days. Still, it was tidy, and the front lawn was cut short.

I had Mindy park down the street a little so we could watch for a minute and see if there was anyone about.

'I don't see his bins,' Mindy pointed out.

I didn't either, but then he wasn't here to put them out. 'I guess they'll be around the back. I'll go find them; you don't want to go through his trash anyway, I'm sure. You walk Buster and keep an eye out for ... well, anything. If you see neighbours' curtains twitching, let me know.'

'I'll call you,' she promised, and we set off. Mindy going first with Buster, and me doing my best to act naturally as I turned up his driveway and went straight down the gap between his house and the detached garage.

My heart started to pound in my chest again. What the heck was I doing? I felt like I ought to run back to the car, go back to the boutique and focus on the things I am good at. However, when I got to the two wheelie bins parked around the back of his house, I knew I was going to at least take a look.

Telling myself I needed to see this through for all the reasons I'd already listed, I flipped the first bin open and pulled out a black sack.

It was tied at the top, but as I pulled it clear, which at my height required me to get my arm way above my head, the bottom of the bag gave out and the contents poured to the ground. On the way there, they ejected various liquids, semi-solids, and things that were sticky onto my boots and skirt.

I jumped back but not nearly fast enough to get covered in all manner of grungy, horrible gunk.

Horrified and wide-eyed, I said, 'Ewwww,' and did a little dance because I wanted it all off me and didn't have anything with which to clean myself.

There was something that was probably yoghurt stuck to my left shoe and what appeared to be soggy cereal stuck to the hem of my skirt.

Looking around in what felt like futile hope, I found a shrub with some broad leaves. It was the best I could do, and they were effective at getting the soggy cereals off at least.

I was so preoccupied by trying to de-gunk myself, I failed to hear someone unlocking the backdoor from inside.

From the corner of my eye, I saw the back door swing open. I swear my heart simply stopped beating and I could feel the colour drain from my face as the horror of getting caught hit me like a wrecking ball.

At once I felt sick and weak and wished I'd chosen to just stay at home today. Who on Earth was in John Ramsey's house? Was it the police? Shane said the chief inspector would be watching me. Had Quinn anticipated that I would come here? Or was it one of John's relatives? I didn't think his parents were still alive but maybe he had a sibling who was now left with the task of sorting their dead brother's estate.

'Are you all right, Auntie?' asked Mindy as the door swung wide enough to reveal who was behind it.

Buster barked, '*We found a key.*'

Unable to believe my eyes, I gasped, 'Mindy, what are you doing in there? You've broken in!'

'No, Auntie, we used a key. It was under a rock by the door. Everyone hides a key in case they lose theirs. Did you have any luck with the rubbish bags?' she asked, then cast her eyes down to my skirt and boots.

She curled her lip in disgust. 'I bet there's something we can use to clean that off in here,' she started backing into the kitchen again, but Buster was trying to get outside.

'*Are those frosted wheats?*' he wanted to know, his little eyes locked on the mess strewn across the ground. '*Ooh,*' he sniffed the air. '*No don't move. That's cherry yoghurt on your boot. I'll get that off for you.*'

I wanted to get Mindy out of the house before the cops showed up. One of the neighbours was bound to have seen her going through the front door. That was going to have to wait though because my dog with a bowling ball where his brain should be was going to eat all the trash if he got even half a chance.

'Oh, no you don't Buster,' I moved to get in his way and grabbed his lead. Of course, now I was close enough for him to sample the treats stuck to my clothing and shoes and I was trying to take my next step with one of my feet firmly stuck in his mouth.

Buster said, '*Mmmmmffll mmugh.*'

'Get off, Buster!' Too late, I slipped and lost my balance as he licked my boot ever so delicately but with much determination. Arms pinwheeling, I toppled and fell backward. There being nothing but free air to grab, I stopped only when my butt hit the ground.

Except it didn't hit the ground because life is not like that. No, I landed back on top of the pile of sticky, gunky, slimy trash that emptied itself from the black sack and now I was truly covered.

Mindy had let go of the lead the moment I grabbed it and reappeared in the doorway now holding a roll of kitchen towel. Her triumphant expression soured instantly because a few squares of absorbent tissue were no longer good enough for the task.

What I needed was a jet wash and a change of clothes.

Buster was making 'nom nom' noises as he hungrily vacuumed up everything he could identify as probably edible.

Trying to keep my rage in check, I grabbed his collar and used his body weight as an anchor to get back to my feet.

'Felicity is not pleased, Buster,' I pointed out as I started to drag him toward the house.

He gave me a quizzical look. *'Huh? You found food. You should be over the moon. Finding food always makes me happy.'*

'Get in the house.' I gave his backside a shove and finally inside, I pushed the door closed.

Mindy was staring at me with a look I might reserve for a shoe if I accidentally stepped in something unmentionable.

'You don't smell too good, Auntie,' she was good enough to let me know with a wrinkle of her nose as she backed away.

Buster licked my bottom.

'Mmmm, chip shop chips,' he delighted in identifying. *'And I think this might be custard.'*

I swiped at his nose to get him away and shifted to stand in the middle of the room. Huffing out a disbelieving breath that my day had come to this, I started to strip.

'Mindy, can you see if there is a black sack under the sink or in one of these cupboards, please. I'll have to wash this lot at home and then see what the dry cleaners can do.'

'What are you going to do about clothes?' she asked while rummaging.

'I'll have to see what I can 'borrow' from John's wardrobe. He must have an old pair of jogging bottoms or something.' Anything would do so long as I didn't have to walk back to the car in my cotton knickers.

Mindy found a roll of black sacks, the same as the one I foolishly took from the bin, and ripped one off. I stuffed my boots in it.

While I rolled up my lovely rainmac and stuffed it into the sack, Mindy left the kitchen heading for the front of the house. Her voice echoed back, 'I'll see if I can find something for you to put on.'

A few more frosted wheats fell to the kitchen tile when I turned my skirt around to inspect the back of it. Buster made to dive forward, but stopped when I snapped, 'No! Naughty, Buster. Look what happened to Felicity's clothes.'

Buster sat back on his haunches and tilted his head. '*I thought you might like to know there is some of that corticosteroid cream in the house.*'

The news stopped me dead in my tracks. 'There is?'

'*I can smell it,*' he boasted.

Frowning at him, I had to ask, 'How do you know what it smells of?'

Buster wagged his tail. '*I'm a dog. That's my job.*' It appeared to be the only explanation I was going to get but it was also good enough to prompt my next question.

'Where?'

Buster got back to his feet and started toward the front of the house where the front door and foot of the stairs met at the end of a narrow corridor.

Mindy reappeared before we got two feet, an excited/amused expression on her face. She made urgent gestures for me to follow.

'Come on, Auntie. You have to see this!'

I had no idea what 'this' might be, but Mindy wasn't waiting to explain. She was already running back up the stairs and Buster was right behind her.

I stared open-mouthed for many seconds before I found the power to speak.

Mindy was staring too, but she was mostly staring at me to revel in my reaction.

She said, 'I know, right?'

We were stood in front of an ornate wardrobe in one of John's back bedrooms. It was a cream colour with ornate scrollwork around the edges and two doors that opened from the centre. The piece of furniture was not what had our attention though, it was the contents.

John liked to play dress up.

In ladies' clothes.

Thirty or more outfits were stuffed into the wardrobe. One was an ornate ballgown that someone attending a ball two hundred years ago might have worn. On inspection, I found it came with a matching parasol. A pink PVC catsuit was next to it. I didn't want to think about what purpose the zip running in a straight line up the cleft of the suit's bottom might have.

Mindy held up another hanger. 'I think this might be my favourite,' she giggled.

It was a naughty French maid outfit with a black silk top, a matching black feather duster and a badge that bore the legend 'I like to be spanked!'.

You might be questioning whether he had a girlfriend, and these were hers, but not unless his girlfriend was over six foot tall and had shoulders

twice the width of mine. Also, most of the outfits bore the same label –
Hers for Him – inside the collar. I thought that was a bit of a giveaway.

John's dressing up habits were not germane to the case. At least, I
didn't think they were and though I needed clothes and had access to a
wardrobe of items that were at least intended to be feminine, I doubted
anything would even nearly fit me. It's one thing to put a safety pin in a
skirt when it's a size too big. Another thing entirely when it will go around
you twice.

We had already been in John's house too long, which was a redundant
statement considering we were not supposed to be in it at all.

Spying something that might work, I snagged a rainmac, the type a
stereotyped flasher would wear. It swamped me, but if I cleaned my boots
off, it might not look too strange. Using the belt it came with, I tightened
it to my body and got back to what I ought to be doing.

Striding for the back bedroom door, I called, 'Show me where the
cream is, Buster.'

I got a woof in response and let him lead me through the upstairs of
the house and into what had to be the master bedroom.

Mindy asked, 'Did he just answer you, Auntie?'

I'd done it again! I would take Buster to the boutique most days, but I
guess I am used to acting in a certain way in that environment, and now
out of it, I was failing to hide my secret.

'Because it sounded like you gave him an instruction and he replied,'
Mindy added.

We were in the master bedroom now where there was no way to
prevent Mindy seeing my expression as I fought for something to say.

Buster wagged his tail. *'Go on, tell her,'* he suggested.

'Um, it's just coincidence,' I lied.

Buster nudged at a bedside cabinet with his nose. *'It's in here.'*

Mindy's sceptical frown changed not one bit when I opened the cupboard and took out a tub of corticosteroid cream. It was the same brand as Joanne had in her hands earlier at the hospital, just a smaller version.

What did this tell me?

'Auntie!' snapped Mindy, which startled me into meeting her eyes. 'How did you know to look in there for the cream?'

Now I was caught. 'Just a wild hunch,' I lied again. 'Buster was sniffing around so I followed him.'

She shook her head. 'Oh, no you didn't. You told him to show you where the cream was and that means you had to know it was here. How did you know that?' Did Buster tell you because he could smell it?'

I forced myself to chuckle. 'How could Buster tell me? He's a dog.'

Buster woofed. *'That's right, I am. Not just a dog though, I am Adventure Dog, scourge of villains everywhere, harbinger of doom for criminals, the bringing of pain for any miscreants stepping outside of the law.'*

'We're outside the law, Buster,' I snapped. 'We just broke into someone's house.'

Mindy gasped. This time, on edge because I was wearing a transvestite's rainmac, standing in the master bedroom of a house I had technically broken into, and deprived of sleep, I had talked to Buster right in front of my niece.

'You just heard what he was thinking, didn't you!' Her eyes couldn't get any wider without her eyeballs popping out.

My brain raced; there had to be a way to laugh this off as my little joke, but if there was, I couldn't see it fast enough.

Flummoxed, I sat on the bed. 'I can only hear him and Amber,' I admitted. 'It's not all animals, just my own.'

'Oh, my goodness,' squeaked Mindy. 'How?'

I snorted a wry laugh. 'I have no idea.' Buster stood on his back legs to snuffle my hand in support. I felt like I was at an AA meeting or something and getting the cathartic buzz of finally confessing my shame. 'It started when I was little. I think I have always been able to do this but only with the animals closest to me. My parents got rid of our pets when I was very small because I used to talk to them all the time. They thought I was pretending. So did your mum.'

'So mum can't do this too?'

I skewed my lips to one side. 'I don't think so. If she can, then she has been lying about it for a long time.'

Mindy came around the bed. I thought she was coming to see Buster, but she jerked to a stop and darted to the window. The suddenness of her movements put me on alert.

'There's someone at the car,' Mindy murmured, staring intently down the road.

I was up and on my feet in a heartbeat, racing to stand beside my niece at the window. True to her word, a man was at her car, his hands cupped around his face as he peered through the driver's window. He was average height and build, in his early forties with thinning dark brown hair. Dressed in an everyday outfit of dark jeans, running shoes, and a waist-length black leather jacket, he could be anyone.

Mindy said, 'Maybe it's the man from the black BMW.'

I couldn't say one way or another. 'I don't recognise him, whoever he is.'

Buster put his front paws on the wall but was still too short to look out of the window. '*Pick me up so I can see.*'

I snorted a laugh. I could pick Buster up, but I avoided doing so for fear I will snap my spine one day. He is like lifting a dead weight.

The man turned away from the car and looked up at the house. Mindy and I both ducked even though I felt certain he couldn't see us through the net curtain. Now peering over the edge of the windowsill like children, we watched him coming toward the house.

Mindy squeaked, 'Auntie, what do we do?'

My heart had begun to race again. This was yet another twist to the mystery. Who the heck was this guy? He clearly knew who we were and whether he was the man in the black BMW or not, he was here snooping on us.

'He's coming up the drive!' hissed Mindy.

Buster started back toward the landing and the stairs. '*Don't worry ladies. It's fighting time. I'll get this one.*'

147

I lunged across the room, grabbing hold of his tail to stop him. 'This is not the time to attack someone, Buster,' I whispered for fear my voice would be heard outside. 'We can just wait in here for a few minutes. He'll probably just go away, and we can leave then. Or maybe he'll wander around the back and we can sneak out the front and leg it to the car.'

'That sounds like a plan,' said Mindy, still peering down through the window.

The noise we heard next changed that plan fast.

'Did you leave the front door unlocked?' I squeaked in fear as we heard it open.

Mindy had a hand over her mouth and a look of horror in her eyes. 'I think I left the key in the lock,' she gasped.

Buster was still facing the bedroom door, my hand on his tail the only thing holding him in check.

'*Is it fighting time now?*' he asked. '*Cornered. No way out. Badly outnumbered. It's time for Adventure Dog to kick some butt.*'

'Um, he's the one who is outnumbered,' I pointed out. 'There're three of us.'

Buster glared at the stairs. '*Semantics. I think the record can show there was a numerical disadvantage. That will be enough detail. Now let me go and try to be brave while I face down the horde courageously so you can escape.*'

A man's voice rang out from downstairs. 'Hello?'

Getting to my feet, I said, 'Dog, you really do talk a lot of twaddle. Mindy, get his back end.'

Using his tail, because it was still the only bit I had hold of, I dragged Buster back a yard and hooked my arms around his chest. He was going to bark in protest, so I clamped a hand over his mouth, getting righteously slobbered in the process. Behind me Mindy looped her arm around his waist.

'What are you doing?' Buster wanted to know.

'Hiding,' I whispered. 'Keep quiet.'

'Adventure dog does not hide. Not unless he is about to surprise ambush someone.'

'That's exactly what I have planned,' I hissed next to Buster's ear to keep him calm. I was a terrible liar, but the dog would have struggled to free himself if I hadn't come up with something.

We tiptoed across the bedroom until I could peek around the doorframe. We could hear the man moving around downstairs. It sounded like he was in the kitchen. My heart sunk again as I remembered that was where I'd left my stinking clothes.

Mindy leaned close to my head to whisper, 'He's going to find us, Auntie. Maybe I should just take him out. I'm not really dressed for it, but if I hitch my skirt up, I should be able to kick properly.'

Buster agreed. *'Yeah. We can tag-team him. You go high and I'll go low. He won't know what hit him.'*

'Good grief,' I muttered quietly. Both my sidekicks wanted to opt for violence first.

Mindy asked, 'What? Did Buster just tell you something?'

'Only that he agrees with your plan to knock out the man downstairs.' Before she could start hitching up her skirt – quite what the man would make of it when my nineteen-year-old niece ran at him with her knickers on display, I did not wish to consider – I cut her off. 'He might be armed, Mindy. Did you think of that?'

'Sure, Auntie. I'm armed too.'

I swore in my head and remembered the pair of batons she pulled from the small of her back a week ago. At the time, someone we thought might be a killer was trying to get away and my death-defying niece stopped her.

'Or he might just be a neighbour. We are not going to beat him up. I already have the police watching me.'

Mindy giggled. 'This is so cool.'

I did not agree, but time for further conversation was lost because we heard his feet on the stairs.

Holding my breath and fighting to keep hold of Buster as he wriggled to get free, I backed us into the master bedroom again.

The man called out again. 'Hello? Anyone here?'

'There's no way out, Auntie,' hissed Mindy, her face right next to my ear.

I worried she was right. I had the cream as evidence – of a sort – but there had been no chance to inspect the rest of the house. I'd hoped to find John's computer and for there to be notes written on a pad to tell me what was going on. No chance of that now.

With my heart thumping in my chest, I snuck a glance around the doorframe. The man had his back to us, looking in through the bedroom at the back where he must now be able to see the open wardrobe full of man-sized ladies' clothes.

Mindy saw him too but unlike me, she made a decision and reacted.

'Here, hold Buster,' she whispered as she thrust the rear end of my dog at me. She was already running by me and into the upstairs landing when the full weight of my bulldog hit me.

I still had him by his chest and the sudden imbalance was too much for my slight frame to hold. Falling to the side with Buster beneath me, I got to see Mindy's bottom as she yanked her pencil skirt up around her waist.

The man sensed or heard her coming. Or perhaps just heard me doing a bad job of keeping quiet as I fell on top of Buster, but he was starting to turn around when Mindy got to him.

His eyes went wide in surprise about a half second before Mindy kicked him in his ribs. His feet were still facing into the room – only his top half was twisted to look at my niece, but the effect would have been much the same no matter which way he might have been standing.

Catapulted into the room, the average looking man bounced along the carpet and sprawled in a heap against the far wall. Mindy yanked the door shut.

'Quick, Auntie! Leg it!'

How did my life get to this point? Barefoot, wearing an oversize rainmac and winded from falling on top of Buster, I nevertheless did as suggested and ran for it.

'*I could have taken him out,*' growled Buster. '*Adventure Dog needs to express his dark nature.*' He stopped at the back bedroom door to bark at it.

'What's he saying?' asked Mindy, holding the door shut.

I ran down the stairs, tugging at Buster's lead to make him follow me, but managed to answer her question, 'Nothing sensible.'

With another, more determined yank on his lead, I got the daft dog to follow me. Once I was near the bottom of the stairs, Mindy started to follow. Less than half my age with legs several inches longer, she caught me in seconds.

Also, I went down the drive to the pavement before turning left to run along the road. Mindy cut a diagonal across the garden and flipped over the wall at the front in a kind of sideways somersault which landed her on her feet facing the right way and somehow already running.

I risked a glance back at the house but of the man there was no sign. Not yet at least.

'See, Auntie!' yelled Mindy. She was about to get to her car, the lights on it flashing as she operated the central locking, but her right arm was pointing across the street. Fifty yards back was a black BMW.

Maybe it was the same one. Maybe it wasn't. I wasn't going to hang around to find out. Mindy was in her seat and had the engine started before I got to the car. Buster had me running faster than my legs wanted to go and bits of gravel on the pavement were biting into the delicate soft soles of my feet.

I didn't try to reel him in though, I egged him on instead. At the car, I ripped the door open and dived in. Feeling like I had the devil himself chasing me, I wasn't going to fiddle around getting Buster's harness attached. He piled in on top of me and with a yank of the door to get it closed, Mindy was burning rubber.

She didn't pick a straight line though. She stomped on the accelerator and spun her steering wheel so the back end got thrown out. My face hit the passenger's window and stuck there as centrifugal force made it feel ten times heavier than normal.

Abruptly, we were facing the other way and Mindy's car fishtailed as she powered it down the street. I thought we were going to get away, but no sooner were we moving than we were stopping again.

Not yet wearing my seatbelt, I got thrown forward in my seat. Fortunately, with Buster on my lap – squashing me with his bulk – I merely bounced off him.

'What are you doing?' I begged to know as I righted myself and fumbled for the seatbelt.

Mindy was opening her door, but paused to explain, 'Making sure he doesn't follow us.' With a flick of her hand, a butterfly knife shot out of its handle, the blade rotating around to face outwards.

She was parked right next to the black BMW and before I could question how certain she was it belonged to the man who'd been following us, she hung out of her door and thrust the blade through the sidewall of a tyre.

An outrushing of air accompanied the sight of the black car leaning awkwardly to one side as its front right tyre deflated. Then, with another flick of her wrist, the blade went back into the handle of the knife and her car took off like a tiger with its tail on fire once more.

Mindy cackled in delight. 'This is so much better than planning weddings, Auntie. We should do this all the time.'

I doubted I could survive a week of this, and as I sunk into my seat and held onto Buster, the sick feeling returned. With my eyes closed against the horror my brain had just delivered, I said, 'Mindy, my clothes are still in John's house.'

My pulse returned to a more normal rate a minute or so later. Mindy was driving at a sensible speed, largely at my insistence, but also because I played along with her desire to be a spy or a sleuth or something and convinced her we needed to be invisible.

My boots, coat, and skirt were inside John Ramsey's house – was that a problem? Probably. If the police found them, they could do a DNA test and prove they were my clothes. That I felt sure of. If the chief inspector was looking for a way to even the score with me, I was making it easy for him.

I still felt sick from the worry of it.

'Where to now, Auntie?' Mindy asked. Before I could answer, she thought of something else to ask me. 'You were looking for Amber earlier at the print shop, weren't you?'

She was bright enough to have put it together. I nodded. 'I dropped her off first thing this morning so she could spy on them and let me know what was going on there.'

Mindy gasped with excitement. 'Oh, my goodness! That is so clever. You've got a spy cat!'

'*And an Adventure Dog!*' barked Buster.

Mindy gasped, 'We need to go back and find out what she knows.' My niece was completely overawed by her day.

I sighed, utterly defeated by my morning. 'I think we need to collect her and go to my house. I need to get a shower and put on some of my own clothes. After that, I need to go back to the boutique and stop

155

pretending to be a private investigator. I'm a wedding planner and I should stick to what I know.'

Mindy looked heartbroken. 'But Auntie this has been so much fun. I thought we needed to solve the case so we could clear your name and get one over on the chief inspector and that man you don't like.'

'Vince,' I reminded her of his name. 'That was the plan,' I admitted. 'It just wasn't a very clever one. I need to stick to what I am good at. All this snooping around is going to give me a heart attack.'

'But ...'

'No.' I put hard emphasis on the word. 'Please take me home, Mindy. I will get my car and meet you at the Boutique. I can arrange for the Escort to be collected from Aylesford and will find Amber. Justin will have work for you.'

Mindy bit her lip, wanting to argue but knowing she shouldn't.

My phone rang, interrupting any chance she had to argue further.

I didn't recognise the number, so when I answered it, I said, 'Felicity Philips, professional wedding planner to the stars. How may I help you?' I flicked the speaker button so Mindy could learn from me as I spoke with a client.

I got a beat of silence from the other end before a familiar voice said, 'Mrs Philips.'

A ball of fear filled my core instantly. The chief inspector was calling, and his voice bore a tone that made him sound like a snake talking to a mouse.

'Yes,' I replied, but my voice caught, and the response came out as a squeak.

'I have an officer at the house of John Ramsey in Godmersham,' I closed my eyes and prayed. 'He reports that he was assaulted by a middle-aged, petite lady. She had black hair and was accompanied by a tan and white bulldog and a young lady wearing nothing on her lower half.' Mindy blushed. 'He further reports that his attackers first broke into a house and he was pursuing them in the course of his duty when he was set upon.' God wasn't answering my prayers today, it seemed. 'Would you happen to know anything about that, Mrs Philips?' he asked.

I remained silent. Not because I wanted to avoid saying anything that might incriminate me, but because I just couldn't make my tongue work.

Chief Inspector Quinn said, 'I shall take your silence as a confession.'

'No,' I blurted. 'It's not what it looks like.'

'Were you in John Ramsey's house?' the chief inspector snapped, his voice sharp and demanding. When I didn't answer straight away, he said, 'Some clothing was found on the premises, Mrs Philips. Can I ask what size you are?'

'No, you most certainly cannot,' I replied indignantly.

'Then I shall guess that it is your clothing. My officer reports that the clothing is covered in food waste, which explains, I suppose, why you took it off. Why were you in John Ramsey's house, Mrs Philips? Are you trying to destroy evidence?'

'What? No! I haven't done anything wrong, Chief Inspector. I was only at the house to find something that would show you what is really going on here. If you didn't think I was responsible for John's death, I would be in my boutique right now arranging weddings. Instead, I'm trying to solve a crime you think I committed.'

With irritating calm, especially given how fast and panicked I was talking, he said, 'Mrs Philips, in the last twenty-four hours, two business partners of yours have suffered terrible accidents and I can place you in the vicinity of both men immediately before they met their fates. You have broken into two properties that I know of and you are now guilty of assaulting a police officer. I believe you are now trying to bury what evidence there might be to tie you to the crimes. What will Derek Bleakwith reveal when he regains consciousness?'

I couldn't believe what I was hearing. My brain was going all swirly and I might have fallen had I not already been sitting. I managed to stammer a reply, 'That I had nothing to do with his fall, Chief Inspector. That is what he will say. I didn't tamper with John's car either. I wouldn't know how.'

We heard a snort of amusement from the man at the other end of the phone. 'Oh, but I think you do, Mrs Philips. Your husband was an accomplished mechanic as I understand it. The officers I have at your house now report there to be a garage full of tools. Am I to believe that in decades of marriage you never once helped your husband tinker with his cars? I'm afraid, Mrs Philips, that I am a very good police officer. Criminals do not escape me, even when they look as unassuming and innocent as you. Please tell me where you are so I can have my officers come to you. Please do not make me chase you, Mrs Philips. It will go so much easier if you surrender willingly.'

I could barely breathe. My vision had sparkly lights dancing in it. He wanted to arrest me again and now he had to believe he had proper evidence. Of course, he could just arrest me for the assault on the man in John's house. It was Mindy who hit him, but I wasn't going to roll on her.

Roll on her! Listen to me. I even sound like a criminal. How long before I am trying to make a shank?

A snort of fear-induced laughter escaped my lips, making me sound a little mad. I wanted to go home, but I couldn't. I wanted to return to work and have all this go away, but there was no option to do that either.

'I'm waiting,' Chief Inspector Quinn prompted, now sounding impatient.

I was going to have to turn myself in and pray Shane could prove I was innocent. What would that do for my reputation though? Primrose would swoop on all my customers the second she found out and I could kiss goodbye any hope of snagging the royal wedding. It felt like everything I had worked for was being crushed around me and there was nothing I could do to stop it happening. Even if I were found innocent, I would be in jail for a period first. Isn't that how it works?

'Mrs Philips,' the chief inspector's voice broke through the numbing fear now enveloping me. 'I grow tired of this conversation. You will surrender yourself, or I will send the full force at my command to find you.'

Opening my mouth, though it felt dry and parched, I was about to say I would come to the station when Mindy grabbed the phone from my hand.

'Come and get us, copper!' she sneered and then thumbed the red button to end the call.

Now staring at my niece in horror, I gasped, 'What did you just do!'

Mindy shrugged. 'Sounds to me like there is only one way out of this, Auntie. We need to solve the case. You said there was a man in the offices last night and he was talking about destroying evidence. There's clearly something going on there. We just need to figure out what it is before the police catch up with us.'

'But I don't have the first idea what is going on, Mindy!' I pointed out a rather large flaw in her plan.

'Yet, Auntie. You don't know yet. We found that cream at John's house. That sounds like a clue to me. Why don't we speak to the doctor who was treating Derek and see what he has to say? I bet if we look under enough rocks, we will find the person responsible for killing John and then the police will have to let you go.'

'But John might have been the victim of poor car maintenance!' I blurted. 'I'm only guessing he was murdered.' A few hours ago, I'd been convinced there was a big conspiracy to uncover. Now I worried the whole thing was in my head. My suspicions were all based upon overhearing one man talking about destroying evidence. He might have been wiping away evidence that he'd been watching dirty videos on the work computer for all I knew.

I was so stupid.

However, I also had little choice. If there was foul play at foot, if I could prove John had a reason to push Derek off his balcony, then maybe I could muddy the water enough to make the chief inspector think twice about locking me up.

'What about the assault charge?' I asked.

Mindy shrugged like it was nothing. 'That was me, not you. Besides, dad will get me off.'

That was it then. The pool of people to look at was a small one: people working at Orion Print, the Bleakwiths ... that was all I could come up with. I added Dr Kimble as Mindy suggested and with nowhere else to go, I asked my niece to head for the local practice in Meopham where Derek would have gone.

Convinced I needed at least some shoes to put on my feet, we stopped first at a charity shop in the small parade of stores that line the main road through Vigo.

Mindy tried calling her dad on the way there, but he was in court and could not be reached. She left him a message in which she begged that he call back as soon as he could. We were going to need his help before the day was through.

Two ladies in their seventies were chatting behind the counter of the shop. They each had mugs of tea, steam slowly rising from them. I was instantly jealous and suddenly hungry. Noon had been and gone which made breakfast a long time in the past. My stomach gave a rumble as if on cue.

'Where do you keep your shoes?' I asked of the ladies behind the counter. They each had silver hair with no trace of their original colour left behind. They wore light green tabards to protect their clothing, which consisted of jeans with a shirt and a sweater and they both looked irritated to have had their conversation interrupted.

The one on the left pointed an arm. 'At the back in the corner.' It was a curt reply intended to make me go away.

That was what I did, finding three shelves of shoes arranged in pairs with an elastic band holding the left and right together. Men's, women's, and children's were all jumbled in together, but I found a pair that would fit me quickly enough. They were a size too big and were cheap knock-off running shoes. They were better than what I had though which was nothing.

Behind me at the counter, one of the ladies was sniffing the air. 'Here, Vera, what's that awful smell?'

My cheeks flushed. I could no longer smell it and had managed to convince myself the scent of John's kitchen waste had faded now that I was no longer wearing the clothes and boots it had mostly stuck to. Clearly not though, for now I was stinking out their store.

Vera wrinkled her nose and nudged her friend, 'It'll be that poor homeless woman, Violet,' she said with a nod in my direction. They thought I couldn't see them, but did they also think I was deaf?

'Look at that coat she's wearing,' commented Violet. 'Maybe the last owner died in it and that's what we are smelling.' Somehow that comment was funny to them as they both burst into a fit of giggles.

Ignoring them and their childish behaviour, I tucked the shoes under my arm and searched through the rack of ladies' clothes until I found something I could wear. Then I went back and switched out the shoes for ones that matched.

'Do you have a changing room?' I called out while looking around.

'Yes, love,' sniggered Violet. 'It's at the back next to the champagne bar.'

Huffing wearily to myself, I bit down my desire to respond and simply stripped where I stood. The clothing rack had ladies' designer label jeans. Too big, but not desperately so, they went on and tied around my waist with a belt. The shoes I found were also a size too big, but they were an elegant brown ankle boot that I might even have bought new had I found them in a store. I ditched the rainmac, snagged a three-quarter length red leather jacket from a hanger, and went to the counter.

163

'How much do I owe you, please?' I kept my tone polite.

'That'll be two pounds, love,' said Vera, her nose twitching as I brought the stench closer to her nostrils.

I opened my purse and took out a twenty.

Both women eye me suspiciously. 'Did you rob someone?' asked Violet. 'Whose purse is this?'

'It's mine,' I assured them, digging a finger in to slide out my driving license.

Both women peered at it. Vera read my name, 'Felicity Philips.' She looked at Violet, the two women staring at each other. 'Where do I know that name from?' she asked.

Violet looked back at me. 'Yeah. I know your name too. What's going on?' They were looking at me with accusing eyes. Enough so that I took an involuntary step backwards.

Vera clicked her fingers and gasped. 'The radio!' she blurted. 'They said her name on the radio. The police are after her. Quick Violet! Get the bat!'

Before my disbelieving eyes, Violet, a grey-haired lady nearing eighty, hefted a cricket bat from under the counter and glared at me with malice.

'Is there a reward?' she asked. I wasn't sure if she was asking me or Vera and I wasn't hanging around to find out.

'Hey!' shouted Vera as I ran for the door, the money still clutched in my hand. 'Hey, thief!'

Bursting out of the charity shop's door and onto the pavement outside, I was already running. I felt like a criminal and had just been identified as a woman on the run. Now I was adding theft to my list of crimes. I might solve this case, clear my name, and still go to jail for the crimes I'd committed to prove my innocence.

'Mindy!' I yelled. She was waiting in the car with Buster, probably having a conversation with him and trying to hear his thoughts the way I did. 'Mindy!'

I saw her look at me and then back along the street behind me to where Violet and Vera were now giving chase. Vera had a golf club above her head and while neither was going fast enough to ever catch me, they were making enough racket to attract the attention of everyone else in sight.

'Stop that thief!' yelled Violet.

Mindy's car was ten yards away. I was going to make it, but as I closed the final yards, a young man stepped into my path.

'Whoa there, lady.' He held out both hands to stop me. 'Did you just steal from a charity shop?'

'Get out of my way!' I screamed, trying to duck around him to get to the car. Mindy had the engine running and was ready for a fast getaway. Meanwhile, Vera and Violet were catching up now that I had stopped moving.

'Keep her there!' yelled Vera. 'She's a crazy killer woman. The police are after her!'

The young man's eyes showed his surprise, and I used it to my advantage. 'That's right. So get out of my way or you'll be next,' I sneered.

He was half a foot taller than me and twice as wide, but with muscle not fat. He looked like he worked in a gym or something.

My threat startled him, but only for long enough for him assess our relative differences in height and weight. Then a smile flickered across his face. He thought he was being a hero and under other circumstances I would praise him.

I just didn't need this right now.

I guess Mindy got bored waiting, because she leaned across to open the passenger's door and that let Buster out.

'*Adventure Dog to the rescue!*' his front paws hit the pavement, followed half a heartbeat later by his back paws. In the next second, he was leaping. The poor young man got hit from behind, Buster's thick skull taking out his knees. The effect was much like watching a human version of an up-and-over garage door. One moment the young man had been an effective barrier stopping me from getting to the car. Now he was a groaning mess on the floor.

I stepped over him and started to get in. 'Sorry about that,' I offered. I held the door for Buster, expecting him to clamber in behind me as he had when we ran from John's house, but he wasn't there.

A pair of screams told me where he was.

He was chasing Vera and Violet.

I slammed the door shut and slapped the dashboard. 'Go!'

Mindy needed no further encouragement, her car leaping away from the kerb and into traffic with yet another blare of horns.

The ladies from the charity shop were trying to get back there but their legs were not going fast enough. Even slow as he is – bulldogs are built for ambling not sprinting – he was going to catch them in the next three seconds.

Perhaps sensing how close he was, Vera abandoned her plan to get back to their shop and barrelled through the door to a local bank branch instead. Violet followed, but as we screeched to a stop again to collect Buster, the scene inside the bank was already one of absolute chaos.

The people inside thought the two old ladies brandishing weapons were there to rob the place! As I yelled for Buster to get his furry backside in the car, the alarm in the bank went off.

How much crazy could I fit into one day?

A lot more, as it turned out. A whole lot more.

Now that I was dressed, I felt better prepared to carry on with what had become a desperate plight to prove my innocence. We were heading for Meopham again where I would find the Bleakwiths' house and the surgery of their doctor.

I was guessing the last part. From my conversation with Joanne yesterday, I knew I wanted to find Dr Kimble. Joanne said he was Derek's general practitioner which ought to mean he worked in the local doctors' surgery. I knew where that was only because I had passed it a number of times.

Mindy pulled into a parking space and paused to think about what we needed to do next.

'Do I still smell?' I asked my niece.

Mindy pulled an awkward face. 'Like the inside of a hippo's bottom, Auntie.'

'Got anything I can use to mask it?' I enquired hoping she might have some perfume in her handbag.

She didn't. A quick root around in her door bins and glove box produced only an air freshener.

It was going to have to do.

It was one of those cardboard ones that people hang from their rear-view mirror to keep their cars smelling nice. It was slightly moist from the liquid scent it was impregnated with. I took off the cellophane wrapper and rubbed it on my neck and hands.

'Is that making much difference?' I asked.

Mindy shot me a sorry look. 'Now you smell like someone stuffed an air freshener up a hippo's bum.'

That was quite enough of that. I was just going to have to smell.

Out of the car, I could already see I had guessed right. A plaque on the wall of the surgery boasted two doctors' names and the first of them was Kimble.

'What do we do with Buster?' asked Mindy, holding his lead.

'We take him in,' I stated, striding toward the surgery's main entrance.

Mindy questioned my judgement. 'Will they let us?'

I was way past caring about the opinions of other people. 'I'm not going to give them a choice.'

The surgery in the sleepy little village was as sleepy and quiet as one might expect. A small dispensary was on the right as we went in. It was closed for a two-hour lunch according to the sign on the outside.

Next, on the same side, was a reception and office area. I could see two women behind the glass, neither one looking excited to have someone approaching them. Beyond reception was a waiting area with several closed doors dotted around the periphery on three sides. The doors must lead to the doctors but there were no name plates to show which one might hide the man I was here to see.

One lonely old man sat reading a tatty old National Geographic magazine. He didn't look up when we came in.

'I'm here to see Dr Kimble,' I announced as brightly and positively as I could.

My smile had zero impact on the sour face of the woman behind the glass. 'Do you have an appointment?' she wanted to know.

I kept my pleasant face on when I said, 'It's not a medical matter, but it is rather urgent. Dr Kimble will want to see me. If you could just let him know I am here about Derek Bleakwith.'

'Without an appointment, you cannot see him. If this is a personal matter, you will need to contact him at home.' The sour-faced woman's colleague was on her feet and peering through the glass. She wasn't looking at me though. Or at Mindy.

'Here they've brought a dog in with them.'

Sour face jumped to her feet. 'Right, that's it. You need to leave right now.'

'I am not leaving until I speak with Dr Kimble,' I stated firmly. She was winding up to start getting excited, but I got in first. 'He's facing a malpractice claim,' I lied. 'You need to let him know I am here right now.'

I could have told her the world was about to end for all the effect I had.

'No! You get out right now. There are no dogs allowed in here! And you do not have an appointment!' Both women were done talking and were now on their way to the office door so they could remove us.

Mindy took a step to the side, whipped an eighteen-inch-long fork looking thing from behind her back and stabbed it into the doorframe.

The door opened outwards and they were trapped inside.

'What the heck even is that?' I wanted to know.

Mindy pointed to the weapon now pinning the door shut. 'This thing? It's a sai, an ancient ninja weapon. Raphael the *Teenage Mutant Ninja Turtle* fights with a pair of them.'

'But you only have one,' I observed.

'Of course not,' Mindy frowned. 'What good would that be?' She reached behind her back and produced a twin for the first one.

That she was my assistant made me shudder.

Inside the medical centre's reception, the two women were going berserk. Shutting them in was much like dropping cats into a bag and shaking it. It did, however, achieve the desired result. Across the waiting room, a door opened, and a man popped his head out.

'What the devil is going on?' he asked. Then his nose wrinkled. 'What is that smell?'

I flashed him a smile, ignoring his question and the caterwauling occurring two feet from me. 'Dr Kimble?'

'Yes?' His eyebrows rose in question.

'Jolly good. I need to speak with you.'

As I made my way across the surgery, Mindy shouted after me, 'Auntie, I think they are calling the police. You might want to make this quick.'

I paused, gritting my teeth. How long would it take the police to get here? Facing the doctor, I took out the tub of corticosteroid cream. 'I need to talk to you about the attempted murder of Derek Bleakwith.' It wasn't an accusation and every word of what I said was true. 'Would you like the ladies to call the police or would you rather they didn't?'

His face turned to thunder. It was not the reaction I had hoped for. 'How dare you come in here and accuse me? Who are you?'

I wanted to answer him with something clever, but I had just spotted something. In his surgery there was a desk with a chair behind it for the doctor and a chair facing it for a patient. Behind the patient's chair was a freestanding coatrack, one of the circular ones, and on it was a single piece of clothing.

I rushed forward to get a look inside his surgery.

I finally felt like I had seen a clue. He made no attempt to stop me, stepping out of my way so I could look inside.

I grabbed the scarf from the coatrack and spun around to face him. 'Whose is this?' I demanded.

He wasn't there though. He was moving to the reception desk where I could already hear the woman with the sour face talking to the police dispatcher.

In my head, two things had just lined up and suddenly I had a motive and a means. It was as plain as day.

Jolted by the revelation, I started running.

'Go, Mindy! Back to the car. I've just worked it all out!'

'The police are coming!' the woman with the sour face yelled at my back.

I had no doubt they were. If she had given them our descriptions, chances were all the police in the county were about to converge on my location. By now they must have worked out that we were in Mindy's car and would have every set of eyes looking out for it.

We needed to get out of the area, but I couldn't do that yet. I needed to go somewhere else first. That belief was cemented when we ran from the surgery building. Right in front of me, in one of the spots reserved for a doctor, I saw something for the second time today. I hadn't realised what it was the first time, but now it meant everything.

'Auntie! Let's go!' shouted Mindy already stuffing Buster into the car.

'*Yeah!*' barked Buster. '*It's adventure driving time!*'

Regretfully, I had to agree with my dog. Mindy needed to floor it.

All Figured Out

The sensible thing might have been to get as far away from where we were as possible, but that was what a criminal would do. I wasn't a criminal. I was a falsely accused victim and one who had just figured out what was going on. Still heading for the Bleakwiths' house in Meopham, I tried to explain it to Mindy.

'This,' I held up the scarf I took from the doctor's office, 'belongs to Joanne Bleakwith.'

'The wife of the man who fell off the balcony,' Mindy wanted to confirm.

'That's right. This morning, I saw a parking permit on her car. I didn't think anything of it at the time, but it was for a golf club.'

Mindy, unable to see where I was going with my explanation said, 'Okay.'

'Joanne can't play golf,' I explained.

'Why not?' Mindy wrinkled her brow.

Feeling clever because I'd worked this out for myself, I told her, 'Because she has a spinal injury from when she was younger. A car accident she said. She couldn't possibly play a round of golf, so why does she have a parking permit for the local club?'

Mindy shrugged. 'She likes to watch?'

I grinned and shook my head, then pointed to a turning coming up on our left. 'Go down there.'

'Here?' Mindy questioned.

The turning was for a dirt track that led through some woods to emerge behind houses on the next street. It was there to access farmland but unless a tractor came along, I doubted anyone would need to use it and that made it not only a great place for us to hide the car, it also meant we could access the Bleakwiths' house without anyone seeing.

'Dr Kimble has the same parking permit on his car. I only noticed it when we were leaving the surgery. He's having an affair with Joanne,' I felt like my big reveal needed a drum roll. Mindy frowned as she tried to work out what that meant. 'You see, Dr Kimble and Joanne want to be together, so they hatched a plot to get rid of Derek. He gives her a cream laced with something that will make Derek's skin condition even worse than it already is and all she has to do is apply it. I guess they were building up the dose until it killed him. No one would question his death because he was so sick and under the care of his doctor.'

Mindy frowned. 'I guess that makes sense.'

'However, in the meantime, John Ramsey, a man we know to have little life beyond the firm he co-owns ...'

'Do we count the crossdressing?' Mindy wanted to know.

I corrected myself. 'No life outside of his work apart from some dedicated crossdressing. He wants Derek to hand over the reins to the new blood so the firm can move forward. Derek refused, they fight about it, and John pushes Derek over the balcony.'

Mindy's frown got deeper. 'Is that a problem for Joanne and the doctor?'

'Yes, because now Derek is in hospital and the doctors there will use the right cream. That's why he started getting better straight away. I was there this morning and Joanne was desperately trying to get them to use the cream she had – the stuff that would kill him.'

'So what happened to John?' Mindy wanted to know.

'I think Joanne killed him. The official verdict is that it was an accidental death, but Vince thinks someone tampered with his brakes and I think he might be right. Joanne is trying to kill off her husband so she can be with the doctor but then John messes things up. I think she was so angry with him, she fiddled with his brakes.'

'I thought she had a back problem and couldn't do stuff?'

Good point. 'Then I guess it was the doctor.' I shrugged. Either one could tamper with a car's brakes.

Mindy repeated her previous comment, 'I guess that makes sense.' She didn't sound entirely convinced.

I knew I was right though. 'It all adds up,' I claimed triumphantly.

Mindy stopped the car when I nodded that we were where we wanted to be.

'So what now?' she asked. 'We try to find evidence at the Bleakwiths' place?'

I blew out a worried breath because that was exactly my plan. I was about to break into yet another house. It was becoming a habit.

Just as we were getting out of the car, Mindy's phone rang. It came through on the car's speakers.

'Dad?' Mindy answered, reading the caller ID from the screen in the middle of her dashboard.

'Mindy, dear. I have a message from you asking that I call you as a matter of urgency. Are you in some trouble?' Shane's voice boomed back at her, filling my heart with hope because not only had I solved the case, we now had a lawyer on our side to straighten things out.

Mindy said, 'Um, I might be in just a touch of bother, yes, Dad.'

I jumped in quick. 'It's all my fault, Shane.'

'Felicity?' He sounded surprised to hear my voice. 'What's going on?'

Feeling my cheeks warm, I said, 'Well, you know how you said I should just keep my head down and not worry about the police?'

'Yes,' he replied in a tone that suggested he already knew where this was going.

'And you said I shouldn't worry about the chief inspector and under no circumstances do anything out of the ordinary today. Just go about my usual wedding planner business and act innocent because I am?'

'Yes.' Shane now sounded like someone dreading what he was going to hear next.

I closed my eyes and admitted the truth. 'I didn't do any of those things.'

Mindy and I heard him sigh. 'How bad is it?'

'We broke into a couple of places, threatened some people,' I started listing my crimes.

'Stole from a charity shop,' Mindy added unhelpfully.

'Yes, that too,' I admitted. 'The chief inspector asked me to turn myself in. He thinks I tried to kill Derek and succeeded in killing John. With the other shareholders out of the way, the business is mine. At least, I think that's his theory.'

Mindy remembered something. 'I assaulted a police officer too, Dad,' she bragged proudly. Then she realised what she had said, and told her dad, 'I didn't know he was a cop though. We were trapped inside a house and he'd been following us around. I was just trying to escape.'

Shane blew out an exasperated breath. 'Okay. I need to get ahead of this and quickly. Did you physically break into anywhere today?'

'As in smash our way in?' I sought to confirm.

Mindy knew what her dad was asking. 'No, Dad, we had a key.'

'Okay, good,' he replied sounding relieved. 'Where are you now?'

'Wait, there's more,' I told him.

'More?' He couldn't believe his ears.

'I know who did it. I figured out what has been going on and why.' I spent the next couple of minutes explaining what I had seen and what I knew. Going over it again, I felt even more certain than I had explaining it to Mindy.

'So now we're going to break into the Bleakwiths' house to find the evidence,' said Mindy when I finished.

'No!' yelled Shane. 'Good grief. Look I'll get straight onto the police. Just sit tight until I call you back. If they find you, let them arrest you. They will do it anyway, but you are innocent and if you are right about Joanne and the doctor then we should be able to prove it. At the very minimum, I can muddy the water and get them to release you. Stay there, do nothing, and wait for my call.'

Mindy said, 'Okay, Dad. We'll be good.'

'Yes, Shane,' I agreed. 'We'll just stay in the car and stay out of sight until we hear back from you.'

Sounding relieved, he said. 'Right. I've got some work to do. I'll call you as soon as I can.'

The call ended and we sat in the car, doing as we were told and staying out of trouble.

How long do you think that lasted?

'That's the Bleakwiths' place right there?' asked Mindy, peering through her window at a house visible through the trees.

I nodded. 'We are looking at it from the back, but I can tell which one it is from the pergola in the garden.'

Mindy wriggled her nose from side to side. 'It doesn't look like anyone is in.'

It didn't, but that was hardly a good reason to get out of the car. However, a little voice in my head whispered that all I needed was one little piece of solid evidence and I would be able to blow the case wide open. Wasn't that what they said on cop shows?

Expressing my thoughts out loud, I said, 'I wonder if the tub of cream Joanne had earlier is in the house somewhere?'

Mindy swung her head around to look at me. 'Or the chemical she was putting in it to make his skin so bad.'

It was a dumb idea. It went against everything Shane had said and was breaking the law yet again, but I already knew I was going to do it anyway. I was going to get out of the car where I promised I would stay, and I was going to break into my client's house.

I sighed and said a rude word but reached for the door handle anyway.

'We're going in?' asked Mindy, genuinely surprised to see me getting out of the car. Getting her answer from the look on my face, she clapped her hands together. 'Yay! Come on, Buster.'

Buster was strapped into his harness and trying to get free. *'There's adventure to be had and you need an Adventure Dog with you for protection!'* His tail couldn't have wagged any harder without flying off.

'I'm not sure Adventure Dog is a great name,' I told him as I unclipped his harness.

Mindy giggled. 'Is that what he calls himself?'

'You're darn tooting,' barked Buster.

I put a hand over his mouth. 'Shhh. We need to be stealthy,' I reminded him.

Buster got out of the car and shook himself. *'The name isn't the problem, it's the image. I need a cape. Might need a mask too,'* he added thoughtfully. *'Ooh, ooh, a theme tune. That would send the right message. All the superheroes on TV have a theme that is played when they turn up. So the bad guys know who they're about to get handed a whooping by.'*

'What's he saying?' Mindy wanted to know.

I started through the trees toward the Bleakwiths' back garden. 'He needs a theme tune and a costume.'

Mindy giggled again, trying to keep quiet but failing miserably. 'Is he really saying that? He's so funny.'

Buster made an audible growling noise.

Mindy listened intently. 'What did he say then?'

This time I sniggered. 'That he is not funny. He is a plague upon all evil doers and a curse to all who would challenge him. He is ...' I tilted my head to look down at Buster, 'Devil Dog?'

181

'*Is that better than Adventure Dog?*' Buster asked with a tinge of sarcasm.

We were nearing the fence at the back of the Bleakwiths' property. Unlike some of their neighbours, they didn't have a six-foot high fence going all the way along. What they had was a post and wire fence, the type that is about three foot high. It would keep wild deer out, which was probably its purpose, but meant getting in for us would be a lot easier.

Mindy crouched down to smoosh Buster's face. 'I think Devil Dog is a great name for you. We'll get you a cape with a great big D on it.'

Buster's tail flicked back and forth like windscreen wipers on fast.

I rolled my eyes. 'Don't encourage him, please. He already thinks he's part superhero.'

Mindy straightened to full height again. 'So I guess we hop the fence. Here, I'll give you a boost.' Nimble little minx that she is, Mindy would get over the fence without the slightest bother. I can still do the splits with a little warming up – a hangover from my ballet days, but jumping a yard high fence with pointy tops was daunting enough that I was glad of the assist.

Before Mindy could get into position, Buster happened.

'*Devil Dog will make a hole!*' he barked. He was ruining our attempt at a stealthy approach, but before either one of us could do anything to shush him or stop him he added some sound effects for good measure. '*Dun dun DAH!*' then he ran headfirst at the fence.

He only covered a distance of about four yards to get there but was moving at an impressive speed when he hit the wooden uprights.

The thing with this type of fence is that it is only properly anchored every two yards or so. In between, the wooden uprights are held in place with thick galvanised wire and it can flex. Which is precisely what it did. Good thing too because it certainly didn't give.

Buster put his head down so the crown of his skull hit the wood. I guess he was expecting it to explode into smithereens or something, but all he succeeded in doing was to shunt it back a foot.

He made a whining noise as he bounced off, and as Mindy and I rushed to him, he wobbled a bit and then fell over.

The daft mutt had knocked himself out.

'Perfect,' I muttered, unable to believe how far I had fallen in the space of a day. Not only was I a fugitive on the run from the police, I was also breaking into yet another house and doing it with a mentally deranged dog.

His tongue was lolling from the side of his mouth. A beetle walked over it.

Scratching my head in disbelief, I said, 'We'd better get him inside. I need to check if he is really hurt.'

Mindy helped me over the fence, then hefted Buster, struggling under his weight, and passed him to me.

I almost collapsed when I got the full weight of him in my arms. Remember I said he was like lifting a dead weight earlier? Well, I was wrong. Now that he was unconscious, he was like a dead weight.

Mercifully, Mindy jumped over the fence like it was nothing and helped me to take his weight before I fell over or dropped him. Just like in

John's house, I had the front end, and she had the back as we shuffled through the Bleakwiths' garden to get to their house.

We were quiet about it, sticking to the trees and in the shadows as much as we could. The sun was already beginning to dip. It was coming up on four o'clock and would be dark within the hour. That made it easier to assess that there really was no one home. Had they been, they would have wanted a light on.

'Let's put him down over there,' I suggested, nodding to the patio behind their back doors. It was right next to the spot where Derek had fallen, and I could still see the scuff marks in the grass where he landed.

That was how this all started. Fate had put me in their house at precisely the wrong time. Change my visit by an hour or by a day and I wouldn't be involved on any level.

Buster started to come around as we put him down. *'Whassa? Wass happn?'* he mumbled.

I was relieved to hear him. He sounded a little dazed, but he was all right.

Mindy said, 'I'll look for a key,' and darted away.

Holding Buster's head and stroking his fur, I asked, 'Does your head hurt?'

He squinted at me. *'Little bit. Did I break the fence?'*

'Not even nearly.'

'Really?' He was both disappointed and surprised by the news. *'I felt sure that was going to work. I bet it would have worked if I had a cape.'*

184

I continued to stroke his fur absentmindedly and looked about for somewhere Joanne or Derek might have hidden a key. There were no obvious flowerpots or rocks in sight. I didn't get to look any further because Mindy appeared at the patio door.

She took a second to work out how to open it, but it swung wide when she did, and we were in business.

'You found a key then,' I said, getting up from the grass.

Mindy shook her head. 'There was a bedroom window open.'

Curiosity demanded I ask how she got up to the bedroom window – I hadn't heard her moving a ladder about, but I parked it for now – we had evidence to find.

'How's my Devil Dog?' asked Mindy.

'*I'm not sure Devil Dog is such a great name,*' Buster admitted. '*I might need to rethink it.*'

'He's fine,' I told her. 'Come along, Buster. Stop hamming it up and find the cream.'

Obediently, Buster the bulldog rolled back onto his feet, gave his head a shake, and trundled into the house. Once in the kitchen he paused to sniff the air.

'Can you smell it?' I asked him. 'Can you smell the cream?'

He sniffed again. '*I can smell biscuits,*' he replied. Putting the task I needed him to perform to one side, he trotted forward until his face was up against a cupboard. '*They're in here.*'

'He's found biscuits,' I explained to Mindy.

'*I need sustenance,*' Buster told me, making his voice sound wobbly and weak as if it had been days since he ate. '*I feel like I might waste away and my nose doesn't work properly when I am hungry.*'

'We did skip lunch,' Mindy added her vote.

I threw my hands in the air. 'Oh, for goodness sake. Mindy, get the biscuits. Give Greedy Guts a couple, but this really is stealing now. We are bad people.' Buster was already slobbering in excitement and Mindy had to shove him back a foot just to get the cupboard open.

'Ooh, *Hobnobs,*' she declared, popping one in her mouth. I chose to abstain and noted that Buster scoffed three biscuits and licked all the crumbs (evidence) from the floor.

'Better?' I asked.

'*Much,*' said Buster.

'Yes, Auntie,' replied Mindy.

Rolling my eyes again, I left the kitchen. 'Buster take Mindy and find the cream. There might be more than one jar, but we can probably ignore any that are still sealed. I'm going to search this place and see what else I can find.'

Niece and dog departed, the sound of them going up the stairs echoed through the house. Confident they would return soon, I started to poke around in the Bleakwiths' living space. I told myself I was justified to do so. Derek had been a friend for almost as long as I could remember, and his wife was not only cheating on him but trying to kill him too.

He had no idea, but if I didn't expose the truth, he would regain consciousness only for Joanne and her lover to find a new way to bump him off. I was going to have to save his life. Little old me.

186

Now, what the heck am I looking for? Feeling like I should have paid more attention to the detective shows Archie used to watch, I regretfully admitted that I had no idea how to search for clues.

There was a computer desk in the far corner of the room. On it was a laptop, a sleek new one. I opened it and turned it on but then needed a password I didn't possess.

How had Vince hacked into the computer in Orion Print last night? A surge of memory had me looking under the laptop for a slip of paper. There wasn't one. I expanded my search, checking under the desk and in drawers but finding nothing.

The drawers were on one side of the desk. On the other was what looked like a filing cabinet. Feeling wretched for snooping even though I also believed it was warranted, I nevertheless hesitated before sliding the filing cabinet open.

The files were the cardboard drop type, where a slim folder, or stapled sheets could be dropped inside. A plastic tab at the top showed the contents of each file. It was all very neat.

I pulled out the first file. The header claimed the file contained 'Expenses'. Inside the drop file was a plastic wallet filled with receipts. It was Derek's business expenses, neatly filed away for claiming later.

The next file as I worked my way back was nothing to do with work – it was their house insurance policy. I put that back and lifted out the next one. It was labelled *Dream Home*. There were cut outs from brochures listing properties in Barbados. I skewed my lips to one side and leaned back in the chair to stare at the ceiling. I had seen a Caribbean homes brochure in the house before but couldn't remember Derek ever talking about wanting to move there.

That was clearly what this was and then it hit me – Joanne was going, but she wasn't taking Derek and maybe she had never planned to. She was going with the doctor!

I put the file back and took out the next one. It was labelled 'Minutes'. It turned out it was the minutes of the shareholder meetings and they went back years.

Guiltily, I knew I hadn't bothered to read the minutes from any of those sent to me in the last decade. Derek always called to invite me to the annual meeting and lunch. I always declined and later he would tell me what happened and what was decided. I think if he had ever asked to buy me out, I would have handed over the shares at whatever price he offered. I had more than made back the small amount I invested to help get his firm off the ground.

I skimmed the most recent ones now for no other reason than because I had them in my hand. It was the same mundane, mind-numbing business I had always found them to contain and exactly why I stopped reading them in the first place. It was only when my eyes caught on Tarquin's name that they stopped to read for a moment.

I had the most recent annual general meeting minutes in my hand and was reading where the shareholders agreed to bring Tarquin into the fold. They were offering him a small number of shares – a big thing for a small business.

Tarquin Tremaine, the man who was, according to John, taking the firm to the next level and who had won Tamara's heart. I was yet to meet him, though I knew what he looked like from the pictures I'd been shown. I could see one now simply by turning my head to look at the wall. Tall and handsome, with a floppy Hugh Grant hairstyle, he was going to make Tamara very happy. Given how well he had done for the firm - I knew this only from Derek talking about him in excited superlatives – it was no wonder they had agreed to give him shares. They wanted to keep him and being invested in the firm would lock him in. That he was joining Derek's family must have made the deal even sweeter and I knew they offered him the shares because he was the one increasing the share value.

Mindy and Buster came back into the room just as I was wallowing in how badly I was letting people like Tarquin down today. I had his wedding to plan, a rush job because of Derek's ill health and ... well, if Shane couldn't make the charges against me go away then they were going to need to hire someone else.

'Found it,' said Mindy, holding aloft a carrier bag with several tubs of the cream in. 'I grabbed some of the unopened ones as well. I figured it might be getting into the cream before Mrs Bleakwith touches it.'

'Good thinking.' I nodded and pushed back from the desk, folding the laptop closed again so it looked as it had when we came in.

Mindy asked, 'Did you find anything else?'

I gave her a glum look. 'No. I don't know what else there might be to find, and I guess I don't know how to find it. I'm not much of a sleuth.'

'Don't say that, Auntie. You figured out about the doctor and the wife having an affair. That wasn't easy to piece together.'

I shrugged in response. About to say something glib, my thoughts were interrupted by my phone ringing. The unexpected and loud noise gave me a start.

Fishing around in my bag, I got to it before the caller found themselves diverted to answerphone, but my adrenalin spiked when I saw the name displayed: Tamara.

Oh, my goodness! She knows we are in her house!

Feeling weak with terror, I thumbed the answer button. 'Hello,' I stammered.

'Mrs Philips, it's Tamara,' she replied brightly, her voice full of energy. 'Um, I guess I have good news and bad news.' I didn't say anything, still waiting for a SWAT team to burst through the window to get me. 'Dad's awake,' Tamara blurted with a gush of excitement.

The news hit me like a wet fish slapped across my face – Derek being conscious changed everything.

'I'm on my way to the hospital now. Tarquin said I should drop everything and just go. Well, actually, Tarquin told me I shouldn't have been in work today at all. Anyway, I thought you would want to know, but I am also calling to cancel the appointment tonight. I'm really sorry. I know we are tight for time, but well, maybe we are not anymore. Mum says dad is much improved and his skin is really healing.'

My brain was asking what Joanne really thought about Derek's recovery and what she might be planning behind the tears of joy she was currently fake-crying.

What I said was, 'That's amazing news. Don't worry about our appointment tonight, we can talk later and rearrange things. If your father is recovering and you want to push the wedding back … we can discuss it all later, like I said. Go see your dad. I'm sure you are desperate to see how he is doing.'

'Oh, goodness, I am. This is the best news ever. I thought I was going to lose him. Oh, I'm pulling into the carpark. I'll call you later.'

I let her go and put my phone away while my brain worked at triple speed trying to formulate a new plan.

Shane wanted us to stay put in Mindy's car, but I knew the truth about Joanne and Dr Kimble and now I had the evidence. What would Joanne say when I presented her with the cream? I'd seen Patricia Fisher mesmerise a room full of people as she revealed who had done what and why. I was going to do the same.

If I could reveal the real conspiracy behind the mystery, maybe I could trick Joanne into telling us how she fiddled with John's brakes to make him crash. The voice I heard talking about destroying evidence last night, could that have been Dr Kimble? I wasn't convinced, but it certainly could have been. I only caught a glimpse of the man as he went up the street, but he was roughly the same shape.

I could do this. I just needed to get to the hospital and into Derek's room without getting caught.

Drawing in a deep breath through my nose as I willed my brain to conjure a plan, I said, 'Mindy we need to find a set of wheels. Can you hotwire a car?'

Mindy burst out laughing. 'Auntie what happened to you?'

'What do you mean?'

She was still laughing. 'Yesterday you were drinking tea from a fine china cup at your boutique in Rochester. Today you are a hardened criminal. I am starting to wonder when you will ask me if I know where to buy a gun.'

She had a point. I'd broken so many rules today, so many laws, that stealing a car just didn't seem like a big deal.

With a little shake of her head, Mindy said, 'There's a car out front. I'm guessing it belongs to someone here because the number plate reads 'B1EAK'. 'If the car is here then the keys must be too. If you want a different car because the police are looking for mine, maybe we should take that one.'

I nodded, chuckling at myself now. 'Good plan. Let's split up and find the keys.'

Caught

The car was Derek's BMW seven series. I could tell that easily enough because the driver's seat was ratcheted all the way back to accommodate his long legs. I had to bring it all the way forward just so I could touch the pedals. I knew the car was something Derek cherished so I insisted on driving – I didn't want Mindy thrashing the gearbox the way she did her own car.

We took hats from the hallway, a black bobble hat for me, and a ball cap for Mindy. With our sunglasses on, it was as good a disguise as we could hope for and I told myself any cops we saw wouldn't look twice at us. They were looking for a sporty hatchback, not a motorway cruiser.

Regardless of the confident voice in my head, I was so anxious with worry that my hands were shaking. I had to grip the steering wheel extra tight just to stop them.

The journey from the Bleakwiths' house to Maidstone hospital took just over thirty minutes. Mindy would have done it in ten, but I was being extra cautious and obeying all the road signs.

We saw police cars on the way, each one making my pulse race even though it was already beating at twice its usual speed. None of the cops looked our way and I had to tell myself that I was seeing the usual amount of police. There were always cops on the road going here and there; today was no different. The difference was me noticing them.

At the hospital that changed, because there were cops outside the door to Derek's room.

We had snuck in through A&E instead of using the main entrance where there might conceivably have been cops looking for me. Buster had to stay in the car. I took him most places, but we would never get through a hospital unchallenged with him at our sides.

Thankfully, Buster thought guarding the car was a worthwhile task and that was how we sold it to him. I suspected he was going to be asleep before we made it inside.

Now we were no more than a few yards from our destination, but there was no way we were going to be able to get past the two constables that stood between us and Derek.

'What do we do?' asked Mindy. 'I guess I could give them a beating, but even dad might struggle to get me off if I tackle two guys in uniform. It's not like I could claim I didn't know they were police officers.'

'No. No violence, Mindy.' I insisted. 'I have broken too many laws today already. This has to end now and if that means I go to jail while your dad argues to prove my innocence, then that is better than you, or anyone else, getting into trouble on my behalf.' I gave her a hug. 'You've been a great friend today, Mindy.'

'Aw, you're my favourite aunt, Aunt Flicka.' She used the name she had for me when she was little and couldn't manage all the syllables in Felicity. That I was her only aunt didn't need to be mentioned. She broke the hug and wrinkled her brow. 'I suppose I could take my clothes off and run along the corridor. I bet that would distract them. You could sneak in then and put the bust on Mrs Bleakwith.'

Her alternative plan was not without merit and might work to boot, but I wasn't going to let her try it.

'Everything all right, ladies?' asked a voice from behind us.

We were sidled up against the corner of an intersecting corridor and peering around it. The man now switching his gaze from me to Mindy and back to me must have thought we looked suspicious, but he didn't look to be hospital security. They wore uniforms and this man was wearing an old tweed jacket that was a size too big and his belly poked through it to force the two halves apart at the front. I judged his age to be somewhere close to sixty though he wasn't wearing it well. He had a light tan as if he'd just returned from a trip somewhere and a knowing look that made me feel like I needed to guard what I said.

Met by his warm smile, I nevertheless needed to get rid of him, but wanted to do so politely.

'We're just waiting for someone,' I told him. Then, because it looked like we were hiding from the police around the corner, I added, 'Do you know what the police are doing there?'

The man waggled his eyebrows. 'I do actually. Apparently, there's a crazy woman who tried to kill the patient in that room. They think she might try again.'

I said, 'Goodness,' and tried to act like the news was shocking. However, though I tried to stop my cheeks from flushing with red, they were doing their own thing and failed to match my words.

Mindy hooked her hand into my elbow. 'We should go, Auntie,' she said with a tug to get me moving.

The man took a step to his left to block my path and raised a hand to demand I stop. 'Sorry, Mrs Philips,' he was reaching into his jacket. From an inside pocket he produced a small black wallet which he flicked open to show his police identification. 'I'm Detective Sergeant Mike Atwell. I'm supposed to arrest you on the spot, but I would like to have a little chat first if I may. Are you going to attempt to run?' he asked. 'Because that would be quite counterproductive.'

My heart was hammering in my chest. I was caught. Remembering Mindy, I corrected my mental statement: we were caught. He wasn't trying to arrest me though; at least not yet he wasn't. He wanted to have a chat first. What the heck did that mean?

He smiled and relaxed his posture. 'I'll take that as a yes. You seem to have caught the attention of my boss, Chief Inspector Quinn.' My shoulders sagged upon hearing the man's name, but my body language just made the detective chuckle. 'Yes, he is something of an acquired taste.'

'He thinks I am trying to kill my business partners. Thinks I already did kill one, actually.'

'But you didn't?' The detective hitched an eyebrow and waited for my answer.

Mindy snapped, 'Of course she didn't. She's spent all day trying to work out what is going on and has it all figured out.'

The detective swung his gaze to Mindy, and then back to meet my eyes, his expression showing surprise and interest. 'That sounds a lot like someone I know,' he commented without hinting at who he might mean. 'So if you are not the killer, who is?'

I sucked in a deep breath and went for it. 'Mrs Bleakwith, the wife of the man in the room around the corner.' Over the next two minutes I told him about the cream and the terrible rash and joint pain, about John arguing over Derek's position and his attempt to kill him by shoving him over the balcony. I explained about Joanne's affair with the doctor and how I thought the doctor was the one at Orion Print last night destroying

196

evidence so the police wouldn't be able to catch them. I had to admit I didn't know what evidence it might have been.

Detective Sergeant Mike Atwell listened almost without interruption. He asked a couple of clarifying questions but nodded along the whole time I was talking. Honestly, it felt great to have someone in the police who was prepared to listen to my side of the story. By the end of my tale, I was buoyed with confidence. I not only had it all figured out, but I had a mature police officer on my side to arrest Joanne and send officers to get Dr Kimble.

I felt like punching the air.

Once I was finished, Detective Sergeant Atwell pursed his lips and scratched his chin. 'I think perhaps we had better speak with the Bleakwiths.'

I couldn't have agreed more. Maybe I did have the brain for solving mysteries after all.

As we came around the corner and into the corridor, the two constables glanced our way. It took less than a second for their brains to get up to speed, their reactions impressive as they both turned to block our path. One was reaching for his radio, the other taking a step forward to intercept us.

The detective sergeant stepped out from behind us. 'Stand down, chaps,' he ordered.

Confusion shot through both constables. They had orders to arrest me on sight no doubt.

'We're to arrest Mrs Philips and her accomplice on sight, Sarge,' the one coming towards us said, confirming my expectations.

'They are already in my custody,' DS Atwell replied. 'Don't they look like they are in my custody?'

The lead constable made an uncertain face. 'Well, they could do with being a bit more in cuffs, if you know what I mean, Sarge.'

DS Atwell acted as if it were an amusing suggestion. 'There hardly seems a need for that, Coruthers. I'm taking them to see the alleged victim.'

Constable Coruthers' eyes flared in shock at the announcement. 'But, Sarge, that's who we're here to stop her getting to. She already tried to kill him once.'

'No, I didn't,' I replied calmly. I felt oddly serene and in control. This was my party now.

The young man's eyes flitted between mine and DS Atwell's. He had orders but his chain of command was not here and a senior detective was. 'I need to check with the chief inspector,' he announced, probably being wise in covering his backside.

DS Atwell continued walking, steering me between the officers with a hand on my shoulder. 'If you must. I'll be inside sorting this mess out in the meantime.'

It was clear the two young men in uniform did not feel comfortable letting us into Derek's room, but the detective gave them no choice. He pushed on the door and stood aside to let Mindy and me go in.

Derek was sitting up in bed, the pillow end of it tilted up to support his back. He shot me an apologetic smile. Joanne was on the far side of the bed, looking our way with a surprised expression. She was holding Derek's hand, doing a good job of maintaining the façade of the loyal wife.

Tamara was sitting on a chair in the corner, fiddling with her phone but got to her feet when she saw us coming in.

She was the first to speak. 'Mrs Philips. The police seem to think you pushed dad off the balcony.'

Derek chuckled. 'I already told them I jumped.'

Theory in Pieces

Like the needle jumping off the record, all the triumphant music in my head stopped in an instant.

Showing my great intellect, I said, 'Huh?'

'I jumped,' Derek repeated. 'I just couldn't take the pain anymore. It was tearing me apart. I know it was cowardly. Honestly, I think I was so delirious from the pain, I never really questioned my decision to jump. It would seem I have caused some drama.'

Shaking my head in disbelief as my well-constructed theory fell apart, I asked, 'Who else knows this?'

Derek and Joanne both nodded their heads toward Detective Sergeant Atwell. 'He does,' they replied in unison.

That Derek had attempted to take his own life was throwing me but that didn't change the fact that Joanne was having an affair and was the one rubbing the deadly cream onto her husband's skin every day.

Feeling my face stretch into an ugly leer, I aimed it at Joanne. 'Does the detective also know that you are the one who created Derek's pain?'

Joanne reacted as if slapped. 'What?'

Derek glanced up at his wife and then back at me. 'What?'

Tamara's jaw fell open. 'What?'

I shook my head and held my chin high. 'I'm sorry, Derek. Sorry that I must burden you with such terrible news. Your wife has been trying to kill you.' The blood drained from Joanne's face. 'The cream she had been applying to your body is what has made you so sick.'

200

'Yeah,' chipped in Mindy, striding across the room to dump the cream on the bed. 'This stuff is eating your skin.'

Joanne looked like she wanted to back away, but the wall was right behind her and the only way out of the room was through all of us.

'No,' she denied my accusation. 'No, I just did as the doctor told me.'

'The doctor?' I scoffed. 'You mean your lover!'

Derek could not believe what he was hearing. Still holding his wife's hand as he stared up at her, he seemed unable to form a coherent sentence.

Tamara did it for him. 'Mum what is she talking about?'

'You almost got away with it,' I stated firmly. 'Almost, but I saw your scarf in his surgery today.'

'Is that where I left it?' she questioned.

'And I saw the parking permit for the golf club, Joanne. The same club that Derek's physician, Dr Kimble is a member of. Is that where you meet each other? We all know you can't play golf. Not with your injury.'

It was clear from his expression that this was all news to Derek; he had no idea.

Not letting anyone else get a word in, I barrelled on. 'The two of you wanted rid of Derek and his chronic condition gave you the perfect opportunity. He was going to waste away, unable to move because of his terrible joint pain. Death would be a welcome release when it came. Daily, you applied a cream that you knew was killing him, all so you and the doctor could be together.' I was almost shouting now. 'Were you going to leave and move to the Caribbean? I saw the brochures, you know. You should have hidden them better.'

Joanne was shaking her head with horrified disbelief; I had her and she knew it. 'No. No, this is all wrong. I'm not having an affair. I don't have any idea what you are talking about.'

'Save it for the jury,' I sneered. 'Derek would die, and no one would suspect a thing. That was until John Ramsey ruined it.' Like a bomb going off in my head to ruin my theory, I remembered that Derek just claimed he jumped. I kept going regardless, now making it up as I went along.

I took a pace to my right, then another, moving about as I watched her and wagging a finger in her direction. 'You didn't know Derek jumped. You thought John pushed him. We all did. But Derek landing in hospital was never part of the plan was it? He started to get better and you couldn't have that. It's why you were fighting so hard to use his cream this morning. You thought John ruined your perfectly crafted murder, so you took revenge by fixing his brakes.'

I turned my head to meet DS Atwell's eyes. 'She's all yours,' I told him with a note of finality.

He nodded his head in acknowledgement, but he didn't move. I expected him to call the constables in, but he remained where he was, watching Joanne. Several seconds passed.

No one was speaking. Joanne's chest heaved from the shock of being exposed for the criminal she was. Tamara's delicate features contained not one jot of colour and she looked like she might faint. Derek was still holding his wife's hand.

Just when I thought I was going to have to say something, DS Atwell, scratched his chin. It was the same thoughtful motion I saw him perform in the corridor outside.

He frowned next and narrowed his eyes at Joanne.

This was it. He was going to read her, her rights.

'Mrs Bleakwith what were you doing at the golf club?

Her cheeks flushed and she looked guiltily down at her husband lying on his hospital bed. The bed she had put him in.

'I'm so sorry, sweetie.' Her voice was a hushed whisper. 'I took a cleaning job.'

I wanted to put my fingers in my ears and wiggle them around to clear out the wax. I must have misheard her.

Derek sighed. 'How much this time?'

'Not much,' she whispered.

He squeezed her hand. 'It doesn't matter, darling.'

Mindy raised her hand. 'What's going on?' I wanted to second her question.

Joanne forced her face up to look across the room. There were tears in her eyes which she refused to wipe away. 'I am a gambling addict,' she announced with shame.

As Tamara rushed to her mother's side and the two of them embraced, Derek took over.

'Joanne has been fighting this for years. It got really bad about a decade ago and she started going to meetings. She even had hypnotherapy to try to control it, but it rears its ugly head every now and then.' He swore under his breath. 'The problem is that it is so easy, and the websites target people they know are vulnerable.'

Joanne broke away from Tamara but kept hold of her daughter's hand for support. 'I took the job at the golf club to make money I could play with. And to hide what I was doing from Derek. We are supposed to be saving to buy a holiday home. That's what the brochures are for.'

'We've been talking about it for years,' Derek explained. 'What's this about the cream though? How is it that you think the cream was poisoning me?'

When I came into the room, I had been certain about all I knew. Now I wasn't sure I knew anything.

Trying not to mumble, I said, 'Well, your skin was terrible, and your joint pain was enough to make you try to take your own life. I thought it had to be the cream. It made complete sense. As soon as Joanne stopped putting it on you, you started getting better.'

Joanne held up her hands. 'I put the cream on with my bare hands. Even if I washed it off afterward, surely it would have some effect on me if there was something in it that was causing Derek's condition.'

To prove a point, she opened one of the jars and smeared a glob of cream up her left forearm. 'It's just medicated skin cream.'

'So who killed John?' I had to ask, utterly flummoxed.

Before anyone could answer, the doors behind us burst open. The person coming in did so with such force that almost everyone in the room jumped, and I turned to find Chief Inspector Quinn glaring at me.

'DS Atwell I hope you have a very good reason for this woman to not be in cuffs,' he growled. The two constables from outside now flanked him on either side and he'd brought more officers with him.

With nonchalance DS Atwell said, 'I've always found it best to only arrest people if they are guilty, sir.'

Quinn's head and eyes snapped around to face the detective in his rumpled too-big jacket. 'What?'

An amused flicker played across DS Atwell's face. 'Well, sir, Mr Bleakwith wasn't pushed. Not by Mr Ramsey and certainly not by Mrs Philips. Mr Bleakwith jumped. As for Mr Ramsey's unfortunate demise, sir, I believe the official verdict is still accidental death because his car's brakes failed due to poor maintenance. Half of the Maidstone constabulary are looking for a killer when no one has, in fact, been killed, sir.'

A muscle was twitching in the chief inspector's jaw. It didn't show, but I gauged his rage level to be somewhere close to apoplectic.

With a snarl, and without taking his eyes from DS Atwell, Chief Inspector Quinn said, 'Constables Romanov and Barton, place these two women under arrest and make sure they are secure.

The two constables who had been manning the door stepped forward, pulling handcuffs from their belts.

A voice rang out to stop them.

'I wouldn't do that if I were you, Chief Inspector.'

Mindy bounced up onto her toes to see over the heads of the officers crowding the doorway.

'Dad!' she cried in excitement and relief.

The chief inspector's jaw tightened as he pulled an irritated face.

Shane begged and pardoned and stepped around and between the officers to arrive in Derek's now almost full-to-the-brim hospital room.

'What are they charged with, please, chief inspector?'

'Do you want a list?' Quinn replied, his expression showing amusement.

Shane nodded. 'Yes, please.' He quickly turned to give me a wink and put an arm around Mindy for a quick hug.

Quinn held up his right hand and lifted his index finger. 'Breaking and entering.'

Shane interrupted to ask, 'Where?'

'167 Mewhurst drive, Godmersham. The property of Mr John Ramsey who I still suspect Mrs Philips of murdering.'

'Ah,' said Shane with a nod as he put down his briefcase and extracted a sheaf of paper. 'I believe you mean the home of Mrs Philips' business partner. I am sure you will concur that there was no sign of any forced entry. That is because Mrs Philips has a key and a pre-existing agreement that she could enter the premises at any time of her choosing. Mrs Philips used to water his plants when Mr Ramsey went on holiday. Isn't that right, Mrs Philips?'

I opened my mouth to agree with his lie, but Shane cut me off before I could.

'You are under no obligation to answer any questions, Mrs Philips. Please refrain from speaking.' Shane's eyes were firmly locked on the chief inspector's when he asked, 'Anything else?'

Quinn extended his next finger and a smile the Grinch would have been proud of creased his lips. 'Your daughter assaulted a police officer.'

Shane smiled back. 'No, she didn't.'

Quinn argued. 'Yes, she did. I can produce the officer in question very easily.' I felt for Mindy's hand and gave it a squeeze. If she was arrested and I got to go home tonight, I would never forgive myself.

Shane drew in a deep breath and closed his eyes. Quinn's smile only broadened.

When Shane's eyes snapped open a second later, he demanded to know, 'Did your officer identify himself?' Quinn's smile froze in place. 'He was inside the home of a personal friend of Mrs Philips and failed to identify himself at any point. That being true, there was no way to know he was anything other than a burglar. Shall I continue, Chief Inspector? Or can we wrap this farce up now?'

The muscle in Quinn's jaw looked like it might explode. I swear, if the top of his head had started emitting steam, it would not have shocked me one little bit.

Without a word, he turned to his left and stormed from the room.

The officers in uniform were all looking at each other, all trying to work out what they were supposed to do now.

Detective Sergeant Mike Atwell helped them out. 'You can go now, chaps. Report back to the station. There is no crime to solve here.'

As they drifted away, the room emptied. It left me feeling like once again I was the centre of attention. I was mortified. Minutes ago, I had barged into the room with a head filled with daft ideas and used them to accuse an innocent woman of infidelity and murder.

'I'm sorry,' I mumbled, barely able to take my eyes off the floor.

I wondered who might speak first and wasn't surprised that it was Joanne's voice I heard.

'I should jolly well think so!' she snarled at me.

Derek stopped her from saying anything more. 'This is not Felicity's fault, love,' he soothed her. 'She got caught up in this and did her best to fight her way out. You saw all those police officers. They have been chasing her because they thought she pushed me. It's all just a terrible misunderstanding.'

Joanne protested, 'She accused me of cheating on you.'

Derek continued to defend me. 'It was an obvious conclusion to draw, darling.' I was not so sure it was; Derek was being very generous.

'I think perhaps, I should go,' I announced quietly. 'I have done enough damage for one day.'

'I should say you have,' snapped Joanne, ignoring Derek and his thoughts on the matter.

'But I want her to still be my wedding planner, mum.' Tamara's hopeful voice startled me. I looked across the room to find her still holding her mother's hand but staring at me with trust in her eyes. 'Can you stay on, Mrs Philips? Dad is going to get better, but I think Tarquin and I would like to keep to the same date if that's possible.'

I looked at Derek and Joanne. Derek gave me a nod filled with warmth and respect. Joanne did not look happy, but she wasn't going to go against her daughter's wishes.

'Oh, all right,' she relented.

It still felt like it was time to go. To Tamara, I said, 'Please call me when you are able to and I will rearrange this evening's appointment.'

The bride-to-be said, 'Of course. I will do that as soon as I have talked to Tarquin.'

There being no need to say anything else. I turned toward the door. Shane led the way, heading outside with Mindy on his heels. As I started to close the door, I could hear Detective Sergeant Atwell inside asking about what else might have caused the terrible symptoms Derek suffered if not the cream.

It was a question still troubling me, but I did not feel that I could involve myself further. Not now. Not after the embarrassment I had just suffered.

Mindy waited for me to catch up. 'I guess we need to put Mr Bleakwith's car back and rescue mine. What do we do after that?'

'You can drop me at home, Mindy. That's what you can do. Then please enjoy a well-earned weekend off.'

'Don't you need me to help with all the things we didn't get done today?'

I smiled. Mindy was proving to be a good assistant. I hadn't expected that. I shook my head at her offer. 'Thank you, Mindy, but they are all things I can manage on my own. You won't get any time to yourself next weekend on Raven Island. That wedding is going to be full on. So make sure you relax over the next couple of days.'

Mindy gave up arguing. 'Okay, Auntie.' We walked in silence for a few yards before a thought occurred to her. 'What about Amber?'

The Truth

At home, even though I desperately wanted to get a shower, change my clothes, get something tasty to eat and maybe drown myself in wine, I was even more desperate to find Amber.

It was dark out and past her evening mealtime. She wouldn't let me forget that and I hadn't bought her a mackerel yet. That was going to result in a hairball finding its way into one of my shoes I felt certain.

When Mindy dropped me at my door, I paused to give her a hug, then ran into the house to fetch the keys to my Mercedes. I also fed Buster; it was that or listen to him howl and whine all the way to Aylesford and back. I only hoped Amber would come when I called her. Otherwise, I might be there for hours trying to find her.

With the dog fed and car keys in hand we set off again.

'*Do we really have to get her?*' Buster wanted to know. His opinion on the matter was in no doubt.

'Yes, Buster. Amber lives with us. I am not going to abandon her in a carpark in Aylesford. Imagine if I did that to you.'

Buster squinted into the night. '*I would be right at home. My natural environment is a broken wasteland. That's where dystopian heroes are bred.*'

'Have you been watching *Mad Max* again?'

'*Little bit,*' he admitted.

'Well, I think you would miss your nice warm bed and the supply of gravy bones under the sink,' I pointed out.

'*Ooooh, gravy bones. Yeah, yeah, yeah.*'

211

I rolled my eyes and pressed the car to get there a little faster. I wanted to have Amber safely back in my arms.

Going slow as I came into the carpark, I scanned around with the headlights, hoping I might spot her straight away. Of course, there was no sign.

I gritted my teeth and told myself she would come when I called her. Leaving Buster in the car in the hope this would be a quick thing, I got out and began calling her name.

'Amber. Amber come to Felicity. Let's go home now. It's dinner time.'

No gorgeous ragdoll cat appeared.

Accepting the need to widen my search radius, I went back to the car to get Buster.

'I want you to help me find her, Buster,' I made my request sound like there might be an 'or else' in the subtext. 'Use that powerful nose of yours and find my cat, please.'

'*Do I have to,*' he whined.

'If you find her, I will buy you steak to have when she is eating her mackerel.'

'*Steak? Okay that's enough motivation.*' He bounded down out of the car, his nose already working. The evening air was cool but not cold. It was many degrees warmer than the previous Friday night at Loxton Hall. Even so, I didn't want to stay out in it for long and I really didn't want to think about Amber having to spend the night outside.

'*I have her scent,*' Buster told me as he snuffled his way across the carpark. Nose down, stubby tail wagging, he led me to the gate at the back of the Orion Print premises. A sense of DeJa'Vu spread over me. This is exactly where it all started to go wrong just less than twenty-four hours ago.

Ignoring the warning voice at the back of my head, I opened the gate and let Buster through.

'Mrs Philips?'

I almost wet myself at the sound of my name being called and pulled the gate shut again as I spun around.

Tamara was looking at me with a curious expression. Framed in the light coming from a lamppost, she was dressed for going out and had her handbag hooked over one arm. In the other arm, she had a small pile of folders.

'What are you doing here?' I asked, shocked to find her back at work.

Frowning slightly as if it were not my place to ask, or perhaps because the question might be better posed to myself, she said, 'I'm behind. I wanted to get some files to work on over the weekend. And Tarquin was working late. I've come to collect him. With dad on the mend, I feel like celebrating. Why are you here?' There was no mistaking the suspicion in her voice.

Footsteps coming around the side of the row of buildings heralded Tamara's fiancé, Tarquin, appearing.

To avoid answering her question, I seized the opportunity to introduce myself.

'You must be Tarquin,' I beamed, giving him my professional smile. I knew who he was from the pictures I'd seen of him with Tamara. They were a handsome couple and no mistake. 'Hello, I'm Felicity Philips. I'm helping to plan your wedding.' I had my hand out for him to shake.

He took it, gripping my hand firmly but not attempting to crush it. 'Ah, the wedding planner. So lovely to finally meet you.'

I froze to the spot.

He had hold of my hand and he was still smiling. I was looking at his face, a face I recognised from photographs, but I also knew his silhouette. I'd seen it going by the window of Orion Print last night, but I might never have worked it out if he hadn't spoken.

'It was you,' I stammered.

His smile turned curious.

The truth of it slammed into me. 'Oh, my goodness. It was you I heard destroying evidence last night!'

His smile was gone completely now. I knew his voice. There was no question in my mind, and suddenly I saw the piece of the puzzle that had been missing all along.

'Mrs Philips!' Tamara's voice cut through the night air. She was angry, and no doubt felt justified to be so. 'Again, Mrs Philips? Did you not embarrass yourself enough accusing my mother earlier?'

Tarquin still had hold of my hand. I tried to pull it away, but his grip trebled the instant I tried. I was pinned.

Tamara closed to where we were standing. 'I believe I will have to reconsider my previous request to keep you on, Mrs Philips. I do not see how this can possibly work when all you do is accuse people.'

Tarquin's eyes were locked on mine.

'I'm right, aren't I?' I nodded as I said it, certain I had finally worked it out. Tarquin had come into the firm and proved himself capable and worthy of being retained. That wasn't enough though.

'What evidence were you destroying?' I wanted to know. My brow furrowed as I tried to work it out for myself.

Tamara touched Tarquin's arm. 'Leave her, darling. The poor woman is clearly deranged. Let's go to dinner. We can look for a new wedding planner tomorrow.'

If I lived to be a thousand, I would never have predicted what happened next.

Holding my right hand with his, he spun off one foot and swung his left fist in a wide circle. It connected with Tamara's head, slamming it backward. Her body followed suit as the power of his blow sent her flying. One moment his fiancée was standing next to him, the next she was in the air, and a half heartbeat after that, she hit the ground and crumpled into a heap.

Tarquin didn't even bother to look at her.

I was hyperventilating already, terror gripping me. His grip on my hand registered as pain in some distant corner of my brain, but it was masked by the horrifying knowledge that I was in the grasp of a killer.

'If you must know,' he replied as calmly as if he were asking me to pass the salt, 'John didn't want his sexual preferences to become public. There was an email chain in which he foolishly attempted to sway my course. I made sure he crashed – all it took was a little nudge when he realised his brakes no longer worked – then I came back here to erase all trace of the crime.'

With a jolt, I realised he was talking about John. 'You were blackmailing him,' I guessed.

Tarquin actually grinned at me. 'It was so easy. Now I can take over the firm. I am the obvious choice to run it and can appoint myself as CEO once I get rid of Derek. How much do you think I should pay myself?'

'What about Tamara?' I whimpered as the pain of my crushed hand began to really tell.

He sniggered. 'That dopey, brainless idiot? She was entertaining to a point. Did anyone really think I was going to be dumb enough to marry her though?'

I was drowning in a sea of confusion. I was arranging their wedding, but he had no interest in the bride? What planet had I landed on?

He laughed again and tugged at my arm. It was then that it finally occurred to me that I probably ought to scream.

I got as far as drawing in a sudden and deep breath, then he punched me in my gut.

I don't know when you were last punched in the stomach. Honestly, I hope you never have been, but the air left my lungs as I doubled over, and sparkly lights danced in front of my eyes as I tried to breathe. I wanted to scream but there was no way I could.

Tarquin followed up the punch by grabbing a handful of my hair. His hand twisted around, yanking strands from the roots to yet again make me gasp in pain.

He was looking around, checking to make sure no one had seen or heard us. 'I think, it's time to go. Wouldn't you say, Mrs Philips?'

If he wanted an answer, he didn't give the chance to provide one. I gasped in fresh pain as he dragged me across the carpark by my hair.

'I should really be thanking you, of course. You coming to me has saved me the bother of having to come up with a way to kill you. Tamara told me all about you trying to solve the case. Well, I couldn't have you somehow stumbling upon the truth, now could I? I was going to come to your little cottage in the country, but this is much easier.'

'Stop right there.'

I got to gasp in pain again as Tarquin spun around to face the new voice and dragged me in a circle with him.

I had to crane my neck to see, probably tearing out even more of my hair in the process, but there, like a knight in shining armour, was Vince.

'Let her go,' he growled, his hands clenching and unclenching with ready energy.

'Who the fruit basket are you?' Tarquin snarled. Obviously, the word he used wasn't fruit basket, but I don't like that kind of language and I certainly wasn't going to repeat it in my own head.

'I'm the guy you really need to worry about,' Vince came a little closer. 'I'm the guy who knows who you are. It took me a while to track you down. I'll give you that.'

I felt like cheering but I was still gasping for breath and felt like my core was on fire.

Vince circled to his left, his eyes on Tarquin the whole time. 'John worked it out too, didn't he?'

'He was a pervert,' Tarquin sneered.

Vince shrugged. 'Whatever. That's really not a factor in the equation.'

'What equation?' I asked. Now that I had enough breath back to speak, screaming seemed a little redundant.

Vince came a step closer. I'd seen him punch people; he was good at it.

Maybe Tarquin sensed the danger Vince presented. Or maybe it was that Tamara let out a little groan and Tarquin knew he had to start dealing with us. Whatever the catalyst, he threw me to the ground, and yanked out a taser.

I call it a taser, but I've never actually seen one before. They are things on TV shows shot in America, or places that are not the UK anyway. But whatever it was, he pointed it at Vince and let it rip.

The things it shot out moved too fast for me to see. The effect on Vince, however, that was right in front of my eyes.

He twitched in place, looking like every muscle in his body had been activated simultaneously. Even though I was still bouncing across the ground and tearing my palms on the rough tarmac, my worry was more focused on Vince than it was on me.

A second elapsed, by which time I was just coming to rest on the ground and thinking about getting to my feet. By then the tasering was done, and Vince folded like a deck of cards. He was fit and muscular and strong, but he was also in his late fifties and I had to question what a shock like that might do to his heart.

Tarquin grabbed my hair again as if to remind me that I needed to worry more about myself. His anger, if anything, had been magnified by Vince's interference and he was being even more rough with me than before.

218

'Who was that?' Tarquin demanded.

'Vince Slater. He's a private investigator. I expect the police are coming right now.'

Tarquin paused. 'I don't hear any sirens. Do you hear any sirens?' he asked. When I didn't answer, he said, 'Then they will be too late. Did you wonder what he was on about?' Tarquin rumbled into my ear; his mouth right next to my head. 'I have made a very profitable business out of taking over other businesses. I move in, I impress them and make myself utterly invaluable.' He was half dragging me across the carpark as I fought to get my feet under my body so I could support my own weight.

'They always want me to stay so they offer me what I tell them I want: a small number of shares in the business. What they don't realise is once you are a shareholder it becomes a game of musical chairs. Do you know how a game of musical chairs ends, Mrs Philips?'

I did. 'Only one person is left.'

He laughed at me. 'That's right. Well done. You are the first person to ever answer that question correctly.'

'How many times have you done this?' I couldn't help myself; even terrified beyond the capacity for rational thought, I was still full of questions.

Tarquin laughed again. We had arrived at Tamara's barely conscious form. He grabbed her ankle and started dragging the pair of us back toward the rear wall of Orion Print. She moaned softly, an involuntary noise that told me she wasn't dead, but she also wasn't really conscious and certainly wasn't going to be of any help.

'This will be my seventh successful take over. I never own the businesses for long. I arrange for the shareholders to meet with untimely, but tragic accidents. Once there is no one left to oppose me, I appoint myself as CEO – that was what John was supposed to convince Derek to do. I got bored waiting for Derek to die, which by the way is a demonstration of my genius if ever there was one.'

Uncertain what he was telling me, and trying to buy another few seconds for someone to discover us, I asked, 'What is?'

Tarquin sniggered. 'The poison in his brandy. It's a delicate blend of cadmium, vanadium, and nickel. It plays utter havoc with the body. As the toxin levels build up, the victim's skin breaks out in a terrible rash and the soft tissue of the joints swell in a painful manner. Blindness follows and then either madness and death, or just death depending on the health and strength of the subject. Honestly, I'm stunned Derek lasted as long as he did. Hence pushing John to force Derek to stand down and appoint me.'

'You're a monster,' I whimpered.

He chuckled. 'I think you mean a homicidal entrepreneur. It's the future for all business. Besides, when I found out about John … well, who wouldn't want to blackmail someone with a secret that disgusting. I even considered not killing him. Can you believe that?'

'How generous,' I murmured.

'One less death, you know – but he decided to get clever and look into me. I found files on the work computer; that was sloppy of him. If he'd done it all at home, I might never have known. Fixing his brakes was a doddle. Just the right amount of turns and the brake fluid slowly drains until … BOOM! No brakes!' Tarquin laughed as if he had just told a joke. 'Soon, the poison will kill Derek and I will be able to buy the shares from the widow or whoever is left holding them. That takes me to the final stage where I run this firm the way it ought to have been. Once the share price is high enough, I'll sell the whole thing. It's a victimless crime.'

'Victimless? You're insane!' I blurted.

Tarquin laughed at me. 'You can hardly count Derek and John as victims. They did this to themselves.'

'And Tamara?' I reminded him about his fiancée.

I got a shrug in reply. 'Casualty of war.'

We were nearing an Aston Martin when Tarquin let go of Tamara's foot. He did so in order to get to his keys. 'Sweet Tamara is going in the river, Mrs Philips. I'll hold her under just to be sure, but I expect she'll be found downstream in a day or so. I'm afraid you will not be given the same treatment. I'm going to have to make you disappear.'

That was enough of a threat to make me call for help. 'Buster! Felicity needs Adventure Dog! Adventure Dog to the rescue!'

Tarquin clamped a hand over my mouth and twisted me so he could look at my face.

'What the devil are you on about, woman?'

We were three yards from the back gate to the Orion Print premises but we could have been half a mile away and we would still have been able to hear Buster's skull collide with the wooden gate.

His thoughts filled my head. *'I'm coming, Felicity!'*

The gate bucked again. It looked old and frayed at the bottom, the lower foot or so rotting slowly from continual exposure to moisture.

'What the heck is that?' Tarquin demanded to know. 'Is it a dog?'

He unlocked his car and opened the boot. I thought he was going to shove me in but instead he threw me to the ground and grabbed something from inside.

Buster's next strike broke two panels and on the next one he broke through.

Even in the dim light of the car park, I could see the blood on his fur.

Unperturbed by whatever pain he felt, Buster barked, *'Dun dun, DAH!'*

He took a half second to assess what he could see now he was back out in the carpark, then he put his head down to charge.

Tarquin was faster.

What he'd taken from the boot of his car was a blanket. Buster ran headlong into it, tangling instantly, and the man I so badly wanted my dog to bite wrapped him up like a gift on Christmas Eve.

I screamed my horror, finally finding my voice. The high-pitched and desperate cry for help might have been heard by hundreds of people or none at all. I couldn't tell, but whether anyone was coming to my aid or not, they couldn't possibly get here in time because Tarquin had just pulled a wicked looking knife from his pocket.

The shiny metal flashed in the moonlight as he bore it high above his head.

I screamed again, and then I heard the voice.

'Hey! Hey, human! I might hate that dog but he's my dog and no one gets to beat on him but me.'

Amber was on top of the gate. Tarquin hadn't seen her but when she landed on his face with all twenty claws extended, he sure felt her.

He made a sound like an operatic soprano being put through a woodchipper as she tore at the flesh around his eyes, lips, and nose.

For a second or two, all I could do was watch in fascinated horror. Tarquin screamed in pain and shock and let go of the blanket.

Without a person to keep him trapped in its folds, Buster burst free and bit the first thing he saw. It just happened to be Tarquin's groin. When Buster then shook his whole body, like a crocodile trying to tear a piece of flesh from a wildebeest, Tarquin's screams not only increased in volume, but went up at least two octaves.

I doubted I could achieve the note he managed to reach.

Galvanised into action – because this was the best chance I was going to get – I clambered to my feet.

Amber was still on his face, gouging, clawing, and biting for all she was worth and once again my heart stopped beating as I saw the knife swing upwards. It was going to gut my cat if it hit her body.

As if watching in slow motion, I saw Tarquin's arm scythe upward. At the last second, Amber pushed off and I had to watch Tarquin stab himself in the face.

My breath caught in my chest as his hand fell away and the knife stayed there. He was trying to look at it even though it had gone into the soft tissue between his nose and his left eye.

I swear my heart didn't bother to beat as he wobbled in place.

When he toppled backward, there was a part of me that wanted to cheer, but a bigger part that needed to cry.

Tarquin laid still. Or he would have if Buster hadn't still been worrying the man's groin.

'Buster,' I hissed. 'Buster, stop it.'

Buster paused long enough to glance at me.

'He's dead, Buster. That's enough.'

Buster spat out what he had in his mouth and licked his nose. *'Yeah. That's right, stupid human,'* he growled at Tarquin's inert form. *'You mess with the bulldog and you get me horny!'*

I felt it necessary to say, 'Um, I'm not sure you have that saying quite right.'

Buster looked at me. *'Huh? Which bit?'*

Amber said, *'This is the part where I get a mackerel, I believe.'* She was sitting behind Buster, calmly licking a paw.

I rushed to her, sweeping her up and into my arms so I could hug her to my body. 'Oh, Amber. Amber you were marvellous. You saved me.'

'Yes, yes. Now where is my mackerel?'

Buster asked, *'I still get my steak, right? I found the cat.'*

Amber turned her head to squint at the dog. *'I beg your pardon. You didn't find me, you flea-bitten mutt. I picked up your awful dog smell the second you arrived. I came to you. Anyway, what is that awful stench?'*

'That's me,' I admitted. There were tears rolling down my cheeks, I was so relieved just to be alive, but my pets were here with me and they were both unharmed too.

Remembering Vince, and feeling bad that I had genuinely forgotten he was here, I found that he was sitting up and watching me.

'You know,' he said, 'I think it's fairly normal for a person to talk to their pets. But pretending they are having a conversation with you is a little weird.'

Champagne

Tamara had regained consciousness but took one look at Tarquin with a knife sticking out of his face and promptly screamed until she fainted again. The paramedics were going to have fun with that one.

The police arrived shortly afterward. Vince called them but they were already en route. Local citizens had called to report screaming coming from our general area.

Vince and I were sitting on the open boot lip of Tarquin's car. I had Amber on my lap and Buster snoring loudly in the empty space behind us. It was nicer than sitting on the ground and the police made it clear they wanted us to hang around. We kind of guessed that anyway.

As luck would have it, one of the first to arrive was Detective Sergeant Mike Atwell, who at this point I considered to be a friendly face.

DS Atwell had news for us. 'I found myself to be curious about how Mr Bleakwith came to be so ill and then recover so quickly. That was your doing, Mrs Philips,' he praised me. 'All that excitement at the hospital this afternoon, well it wasn't for nothing.' He turned to looked at Tarquin's body lying just a few yards away. 'Of course, you were right anyway. There really was someone trying to kill Mr Bleakwith. It just wasn't his wife.'

I really didn't feel there was a need to remind me how much of a fool I'd made of myself.

'It turned out Mr Bleakwith's brandy had been poisoned. It was a very subtle concoction. It was guess work ... and a little intuition,' he allowed himself a small pat on the back, 'that led me to find it. I figured it had to be something he was coming into regular contact with. A short discussion of what he had ingested, imbibed, or absorbed on a regular basis but not

226

since going into hospital reduced the list to just a few items. My guess, for that is all it can be since our suspect cannot answer any questions or give a confession, is that Mr Tremaine dosed the brandy whenever he visited.'

I nodded my head. In all the dazed confusion, it hadn't occurred to me to tell anyone about the poisoned brandy. Now I didn't need to. They would take a statement from me later, and I would tell them everything Tarquin confessed to then.

Two crime scene chaps arrived, tutting and sighing as they circled the body.

DS Atwell turned to observe them. 'What do you think, Steven?'

One of the pair, a man in his mid-forties and difficult to distinguish from his colleague except that he wore glasses, said, 'Looks like a cat scratched his face off.'

Amber said, 'Meowlr.'

Steven raised his eyebrows and snorted a laugh when he spotted the cat in my arms. 'I guess I was right then. Hey, Simon, when was the last time we had a death by cat attack?'

The crime scene man's partner smiled. 'You know. I think that might be a first.'

They were both joking and smiling – it seemed terribly out of place standing over a man who had recently died, but I held my tongue because I could only imagine what death and horror people in their line of work saw.

When DS Atwell excused himself - he needed to coordinate and stuff, Vince took out his phone, shot me a smile, and called The Wild Oak.

'Yes, good evening. Yes, I hope you can be of assistance. You probably heard the police sirens going by a moment ago. Yes, there has been a minor incident in the carpark by the river. It's all over now though. That's why I'm calling actually.' He kept pausing to listen to the person at the other end of the line. 'Yes, can you send a bottle of your best champagne and two glasses down to me. Please tell whoever is delivering it that I have a handsome tip for their trouble. You'll bring it yourself? Even better.' He fumbled in his jacket to retrieve his wallet and came up empty.

Frowning, he mouthed, 'Excuse me,' and darted across the carpark.

Stroking Amber's fur, I watched him reach a car. It wasn't the car he'd been driving this morning though; it was a black BMW.

My mouth fell open.

He jogged back to me, reciting the number from his credit card. He paid for the champagne right there and then.

I had to admit it, it was a smooth move.

When he ended the call, I asked. 'Did you find one of your tyres slashed today?'

He gave me a confused look. 'No. Why?'

'Nevermind,' I muttered. 'You were following me though, weren't you?'

He shrugged apologetically. 'I thought you might get into trouble.'

Among all the other things Mindy and I had done today, we had stuck a knife in an innocent person's tyre.

While we waited for the waiter to arrive, Vince explained what he had been doing since breakfast this morning. 'When we overheard that man

228

last night – we know it was Tarquin now – I felt sure there was something happening that was far more sinister than a man falling off his balcony. When we got arrested because the other senior partner died, it left me with no doubt. I took what I knew and the little bit of evidence I had, and I started to dig. I had to look at all the employees and dug into their pasts.'

I interrupted him. 'I thought the police took the data drive when they arrested you.'

'They did,' he agreed.

Across the carpark in the cut through between the line of buildings, a young man holding a very obvious bottle of champagne and two glasses was being held at bay by a young police officer.

Vince jumped to his feet. 'Won't be a moment.'

He returned seconds later with the champagne and glasses in hand and I had to wonder, as he shot the cork into the night sky and poured the sparkling liquid, if we were the first people to drink champagne in the middle of a crime scene.

Under different circumstances, I might have toasted to the future, but having figured something out, I said, 'You stole the paperwork from my handbag last night, didn't you?'

Vince made an irritated face that told me I was on the money.

'That's how you figured it out, wasn't it?' I accused him. 'You left me fumbling and took the evidence I found so you could figure this out for yourself.'

Vince sucked in some air between his teeth. 'The clues on those sheets of paper ... they were pretty obscure, babe. You were never going to be able to work it out from that. I only got there because I have years of experience in this business and a heap of contacts and resources I can turn to for help.'

I let him fill my champagne glass, then asked, 'Don't you think that is a little presumptuous?'

He held his glass up for me to clink mine against. 'The important thing, babe, is that we solved the case and stopped the bad guy.'

I poured my drink over his head.

The End

Except it isn't. It's the end of this small chapter but wait until you read what happens next! Check the next page to get a look.

Yet again, as I finish this book, it is early in the morning and I probably ought to be asleep. Why did I stay up to finish it when I could just write the words tomorrow? Well, there are a couple of reasons.

The first is all to do with story flow and how I find myself immersed in it. Each morning when I start writing, it takes me a while to get going – I have to find the flow of the story. That is more true at the start of a book, when I am trying to find my way into the story. The way I write ... making it up as I go along, it is very immersive. I honestly have no idea who is going to do what when I sit in front of my laptop. Toward the end, when I am in the last quarter of the book, that is less true. By then, the decisions have been made and the villain identified. By then, I am focused on the end and have a head rush to finish.

That is one reason why I stay up to the early hours to finish a book.

The other reason is the number of readers who tell me they stayed up until two or three or just didn't get any sleep because they couldn't stop reading. It is perhaps the greatest praise an author can get. I write stories that I would want to read and take my time to craft endings that take many, many books to arrive at.

I finished writing this book on the same day that book twenty in my Patricia Fisher series was published. In that book, I conclude a story arc that began in book one. The point is that the stories I want to tell cannot play out in a single book.

What do I mean?

Vince is clearly interested in Felicity. She could be interested in Vince, but I have another suitor waiting in the wings. Will either be suitable to win the lady's heart? In truth, I haven't decided yet. This series will run for a long while, so no decision is necessary. Not before the royal wedding anyway.

In this book I mention houses with ship's beams in them. I believe this is not the first time I have brought the subject up in my books. I first came across a house with a curved beam from the hull of a ship as a young teenager. I was visiting the house of a friend not far from where I now live. Chatham dockyard, responsible for the construction of many wooden warships, is just a few miles to the east. As old ships were broken up, the oak beams were sought after as construction material – waste not and all that.

If I had the chance to buy a property with such history steeped into it, I would be sorely tempted.

It occurs to me that there may be people for whom this is the very first book of mine that they read. If that is the case, you have no doubt been asking who the heck Patricia Fisher is. She's my bestselling sleuth and a character for who I have great affection. Patricia allowed me to cast off the corporate, bleeding eye socket life that I had. She gave me commercial success as an author, and I have never looked back. I have no wish to push you, but if you enjoyed this book enough to still be reading the author's notes, you will love her adventures.

In this story, John Ramsey is belittled for his desire to wear women's clothing. I wish to make it clear that I have no opinion on the subject. To accentuate this, I will claim that the clothing label I use – Hers for Him – is one I invented more than a decade ago when I briefly considered setting up an online marketplace for transvestites, transexuals, and crossdressers.

The idea came to me through a chance observation at a boot fair. If the term boot fair does not translate in your country, it is a place where people gather and sell things from the back of their car – in the UK, the bit at the back of your car is the boot.

Anyway, what I found was that there were lots of ladies' clothes for sale with the labels still in them. Someone had bought an item and either never worn it or was speculating about dropping a dress size to get into it and never did. Whatever the case, I could buy lots of man-sized (if not man shaped) ladies designer outfits for pennies. How much would they sell for to an introverted audience?

I never did find out though I'll admit I remain curious.

Thankfully, I found books instead. Otherwise, I might be sat here in a taffeta ballgown right now.

One final note is to do with the wonderful differences within the same language. In the UK, a house has a ground floor and an upstairs. Or one might call the upstairs the first floor. Any building with multiple floors starts with a ground floor. When you get to the top of the first flight of stairs, you reach the first floor. Not so in other parts of the world. I have to choose my words and construct my sentences in such a way that I do not confuse half the people who will read the book.

In the first draft of this story, Derek fell from the first floor, but my American proofreaders wanted to know how that was possible since to them the first floor is level with the ground.

The next adventure for Felicity, Buster, Amber, Mindy and more can be found on the next page.

Take care

Steve Higgs

Superstar celebrity wedding planner, Felicity Philips has an event to run on a private island this weekend. With a stunning landscape as their backdrop and an architectural masterpiece for their venue, it's the perfect setting ...

... for a murder.

After the nightmare of last weekend … oh, and the one before that, Felicity was hoping for things to run smoothly.

However, an unpredicted storm cuts them off from the mainland before all the guests and staff can arrive. That's a big enough problem for a person trying to impress a prince. But when a guest is found hanging from the rafters, it becomes clear there is a killer in their midst.

Can Felicity employ Buster the bulldog and Amber the cat to help her again? Aided by her loyal assistant, AKA her ninja niece, Mindy, the team of four have no choice but to solve their way out of this one.

A FREE Rex and Albert Story

There is no catch. There is no cost. You won't even be asked for an email address. I have a FREE Rex and Albert short story for you to read simply because I think it is fun and you deserve a cherry on top. If you have not yet already indulged, please click the picture below and read the fun short story about Rex and Albert, a ring, and a Hellcat.

When a former police dog knows the cat is guilty, what must he do to prove his case to the human he lives with?

His human is missing a ring. The dog knows the cat is guilty. Is the cat smarter than the pair of them?

A home invader. A thief. A cat. Is that one being or three? The dog knows but can he make his human listen?

Baking. It can get a guy killed.

When a retired detective superintendent chooses to take a culinary tour of the British Isles, he hopes to find tasty treats and delicious bakes …

… what he finds is a clue to a crime in the ingredients for his pork pie.

His dog, Rex Harrison, an ex-police dog fired for having a bad attitude, cannot understand why the humans are struggling to solve the mystery. He can already smell the answer – it's right before their noses.

He'll pitch in to help his human and the shop owner's teenage daughter as the trio set out to save the shop from closure. Is the rival pork pie shop across the street to blame? Or is there something far more sinister going on?

One thing is for sure, what started out as a bit of fun, is getting deadlier by the hour, and they'd better work out what the dog knows soon, or it could be curtains for them all.

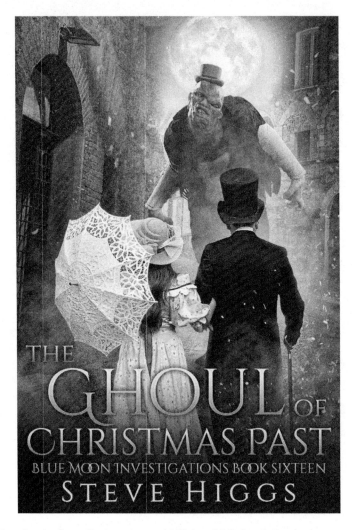

Twas the day before Christmas and Michael Michaels is about to upset his wife.

Recent adventures with his son, Tempest, have piqued his need for a little more action in his life ...

... but when he finds himself facing off against a giant ghoul a few hours later, he begins to think he should have listened to Mary and stayed at home.

In trouble with the police, in trouble with his wife, and generally just in trouble, Michael Michaels knows he has uncovered a mystery, but just what the heck is going on? A theft from a museum, a missing man, and a scary figure lurking in the shadows … what do they add up to?

Michael has no idea, but he's going to find out.

With a little help from a certain bookshop owner and his assistants, Tempest's dad has only a few hours to solve this case. But when the chips are down, does he have what it takes to come up with a cool line at the right time? Or is he just another pensioner trying to do more than his old bones will allow?

The paranormal? It's all nonsense, but proving it might just get them all killed.

More Books by Steve Higgs

Blue Moon Investigations

Patricia Fisher Cruise Mysteries

Patricia Fisher Mystery Adventures

What Sam Knew

Solstice Goat

Recipe for Murder

A Banshee and a Bookshop

Diamonds, Dinner Jackets, and Death

Frozen Vengeance

Mug Shot

The Godmother

Murder is an Artform

Wonderful Weddings and Deadly Divorces

Dangerous Creatures

Albert Smith Culinary Capers

Pork Pie Pandemonium

Bakewell Tart Bludgeoning

Stilton Slaughter

Bedfordshire Clanger Calamity

Death of a Yorkshire Pudding

Cumberland Sausage Shocker

Arbroath Smokie Slaying

Dundee Cake Dispatch

Felicity Philips Investigates

To Love and to Perish

Tying the Noose

Real of False Gods

Untethered magic

Unleashed Magic

Get sneak peaks, exclusive giveaways, behind the scenes content, and more. Plus, you'll be notified of Fan Pricing events when they occur and get exclusive offers from other authors because all UF writers are automatically friends.

Not only that, but you'll receive an exclusive FREE story staring Otto and Zachary and two free stories from the author's Blue Moon Investigations series.

Yes, please! Sign me up for lots of FREE stuff and bargains!

Want to follow me and keep up with what I am doing?

Facebook

Printed in Great Britain
by Amazon

67710040R00142